Dream Ink Publications Presents

For the Love of Money

A Novel by
Courtney Simone

For the Love of Money

More books by Courtney

Love, Lies 'N Betrayal

"There's always warning before destruction"

Love, Lies 'N Betrayal 2

"Be mindful of your actions, 'cause karma is a BITCH!"

Love, Lies 'N Betrayal 3

"The desire for REVENGE"

Table of Contents

Prologue 1

Chapter 1: Scared money don't make money 14

Chapter 2: Go and Get It.................................... 23

Chapter 3: Pop that Pussy 33

Chapter 4: In Love with the Money 45

Chapter 5: Control Your Hoes............................. 61

Chapter 6: Money make her world turn.................. 74

Chapter 7: Take it Slow..................................... 82

Chapter 8: Welcome to the Trap.......................... 89

Chapter 9: Watch ya hands................................. 98

Chapter 10: Don't do this to me 106

Chapter 11: Whatever it Takes 116

Chapter 12: In a Bind...................................... 124

Chapter 13: I don't know shit............................ 132

Chapter 14: Snitches get Stitches 142

Chapter 15: Don't get caught............................ 151

Chapter 16: The walls are closing in................... 157

Chapter 17: When it Ends................................. 165

Epilogue... 173

About the Author 181

Prologue

Three years earlier

Rod walked into the house and slammed the door behind him as he flicked the light switch on and off repeatedly.

"Damn! The lights are off again?"

From the candles that lit up the room, he was still able to see his mother sitting at the table just a few feet away from where he stood. She was already high off the cocaine that sat in front of her on the table, with a bottle of whiskey that was nearly empty.

At that moment, Rod stared at his mother with a sullen look; he was angry and disappointed at how unfit of a mother she was.

"This is why we don't have any lights or food on the table. You go on to spend the little bit of money you have on this bullshit." With built-up anger and frustration, he tried to take the bottle from her and at the same time knock the cocaine onto the floor.

"Go on now! You better stop it now! Leave me and my shit alone."

His mother tried stopping him, but she couldn't. She was moving sluggishly from being so drunk that she was overpowered by Rod.

He stood in front of her for a few seconds, disgusted of what she'd turned out to be. He left her at the table and headed to the back of their tiny apartment where his sister was.

Boom, boom, boom, boom! He pounded on her room door yelling, "Diamond!"

She quickly came to the door, sticking her head out and shushing him, as her babies were finally asleep.

After catching her in the house with her baby daddy, years ago, and ending up pregnant with the twins, he hardly trusted her ass after that. So, he peeped over her head, trying to look into her room. He finally caught a glance, only to find his twin nephews, Josh and Jordan, lying on a dirty blanket on the hard, cold cemented floor. There was just one small pillow underneath each of them to protect their bodies from the pain the floor often caused.

His sister was nothing like the mother that raised her. Being a single teen mom with no job, she did everything she could for them. She made what she had work for survival. She took care of those boys and put them second to none, not even school that she was so serious about.

Although this was their lives and they were getting used to it, it always angered Rod to see them sleeping on the floor, her using lit candles around the house for light, him hearing her cry about how hungry she was, and complaining about her not having shit.

He knew how much he needed to step up and be the man that his father never was. Getting a legit job would take more time than he was willing to spare, so he knew there was only one other option. Never being a street nigga or a problemed child, he was hesitant about making that move. After reminding himself that their struggle was real life shit, he realized he didn't have a choice about the next move he needed to make.

"Do you mind watching out for my babies for just a half hour? I'll be right back."

"Where are you going? It's very dark outside."

"I'm just going to Jeffrey's Corner Store; I'll be right back," Diamond promised.

Rod started rubbing his head, feeling indecisive about whether he should let her go alone or not. It was late, and with the crime rate so high in the city, he couldn't stand the thought of her getting raped, kidnapped, or killed.

"I'm coming with you."

"How? The boys are asleep, and I can't leave them here alone with Ma." Diamond whispered and glanced in the direction of their mother.

"Bundle them up, and I'll grab the stroller." Diamond stood, confused. That wasn't what she expected to hear. She thought she would be able to get away and take a walk to enjoy the cool breeze alone. She never had much time to herself, now that she had kids and was trying to focus on school.

Rod shrugged his shoulders. "What? I can't let you go alone. It's late already."

Diamond went back into the room and dressed her boys right before blowing out the candles. She walked past her mom, as she was still doing more cocaine at the kitchen table and shook her head constantly. *I can't be like that,* Diamond said to herself. She never understood why she continued to do that to herself, and although Diamond tried ignoring it, it was easier said than done. She knew there was nothing she could tell her mother that would stop her from abusing the drugs and alcohol, so the only thing she could do was promise herself that she wouldn't end up like her.

As they walked to the store, Rod made conversation. They had a close relationship, but since Rod was hanging with his homeboys more lately, they didn't spend much time with each other anymore.

"What do you need from the store this time of night anyway?"

"Just a few things. Gosh, you're nosy."

Rod laughed and shuffled around in his pocket and handed her a twenty-dollar bill.

"I know this ain't much, but this is all I can spare right now. I'm trying to pay these bills, once again. I'm not trying, I will. I can't and won't let y'all down."

"Thank you. I only had five dollars, so this will help a lot."

When they arrived at the store, Rod saw a few of his homeboys and went to talk to them until Diamond was done shopping. They went to the corner store often. So often the owner knew them by their names. In fact, he knew their mom as well and watched them grow up from just little kids. He knew she would be good going inside alone.

Diamond walked in the store, still pushing her boys in the stroller.

"Hi, Mr. Jeffrey!" she hollered.

She walked through the store and grabbed the few things she came for: the two packs of pull-ups and a few cans of tuna for her babies. They were two now, but she still treated them as and often called them her babies. She then went to grab tampons, chips, and candy bars for herself. She continued to walk around, looking constantly to make sure no one was near, all while trying not to take too much time or look suspicious. While the coast was clear, she shoved a few things underneath the twins and inside of her bra and underwear.

When she got to the register, she placed the pull-ups and tuna on the counter. Mr. Jeffrey, the store owner, rung up the items, looking repeatedly over his glasses at her while he gathered the items together. She began to get nervous, sweating lightly, and she felt a knot in the pit of her stomach. She tried her best to hold back from giving herself away.

"Your total is twenty-six dollars and eighteen cents."

Diamond put the money she had on the counter. "I'm sorry, Mr. Jeffrey. Twenty-five dollars is all that I have. I promise I will pay you back the difference."

He paused with the bagging of her items, looked up at her, and stared at her for a few seconds longer.

"It's alright, Diamond. Just don't make it a habit."

She nodded and started loading her bags in the basket of the stroller.

"I won't! Thank you so much! You don't know how bad I needed these."

She started heading out the door, but Mr. Jeffrey stopped her.

"Wait a minute, Diamond," she heard him say right before she paused. She closed her eyes, and as she turned around slowly to face him, she whispered to herself, *Damnit!* She knew at that moment she was busted. All she thought about was how much she couldn't go to jail because such a place was no fit for her. Diamond was a softy and would get handled every day in jail if she went. She looked at Mr. Jeffrey with a concerned look.

"Don't think I don't know what you did. I saw you! You steal from me all the time. The only reason I haven't called the police on you is because I know you are a good kid and because of those two right there," Mr. Jeffrey said, pointing down at her babies while her eyes followed his fingers.

"But that doesn't mean you will get this lucky anywhere else. This is the last time it's gonna happen! This has to stop! You better be careful out there, girl, because not everyone will be as lenient with you as I am!"

"Thank you so much, Mr. Jeffrey. I won't do it again."

Rod walked into the store at the end of their conversation.

"What's wrong? Did I not give you enough money?"

Diamond whispered, "I made it enough, now let's go. Hurry up and walk!"

As soon as they got outside the door, Rod looked at her and shook his head. He already had an idea of what went on because she was

5

forced to do it so often, but that didn't mean he approved of it. He wanted to beat Diamond's ass for what she did, but it wasn't much he could say or do to her because he didn't have much to give.

"You were stealing again, wasn't you?"

"I had too. What else am I supposed to do? Before you go off on me, let me just say this is the last time I'm gonna do it."

"Damn, Diamond! You say that every time. You really have to stop with that shit! If you go to jail, I can't get you out. I barely have enough money for what we need right now."

"I know, Rod. It's not like I do it for pleasure. I have no choice. I already said I won't do it again though. I'm hoping to get a job soon so I can help you out."

"No! I don't need your help. If you want to do anything for me, focus on school, and always be good to the twins."

When they got back to the house, Diamond fed the twins the tuna from the can and placed a clean pull-up on them. The ones they wore were well overused, as they began to fall apart. She put the twins down to sleep, and she sat up munching on the snacks she stole. She bit into the candy bar and closed her eyes slowly while the chocolate melted softly in her mouth. She hadn't had a meal since lunch at school, so that Hershey candy bar tasted more like a juicy cheeseburger to her. She knew things had to change because they couldn't continue to live like this.

The next day came, and it was time for Diamond and Rod to get ready for school. He was a senior in high school whose attendance started slacking after he was forced to step up and be the man of the house. She was right behind him as a junior. One of her goals that meant a lot to her was graduating high school and getting her diploma. As hard as it was, she tried her hardest to stay focused.

Diamond went a few doors down to Ms. Mable's, who looked out for her and Rod and watched her kids while they went to school. In fact, she watched and raised a lot of kids in the neighborhood; that was how she earned her income. Luckily for Diamond, she was one of the few that weren't charged. It wasn't like she had the money for it anyways. Her and Ms. Mable made an agreement that she would watch her kids free of charge, as long as she went to school and kept up with her grades. She knew how rough they had it already, so she always tried to help.

Ms. Mable was the sweet old lady who the neighborhood called 'the hood mama.' Everybody loved and respected her like their own. She was nice, but she was hard as hell on all of them too. She wanted them to make a better way and get out of that wicked ass neighborhood that didn't have anything to offer them but a jail cell or a bullet.

"Take care of my babies," Diamond told her.

Ms. Mable looked at her and said, "Now you know you ain't gotta tell me that. These are my babies just as well as yours. Now go on before you miss the bus." Diamond grabbed her and squeezed her tightly before running off to the bus stop.

Shortly after she got to school, she realized she hadn't seen Rod. She looked around for him everywhere. She even asked around, but nobody seemed to have seen him. Diamond already knew he was out cutting school to hang with his no-good ass friends that she hated. All they did was steal, rob, and kill, dragging her brother into all the bullshit they got themselves into. Diamond was the youngest of the two of them, but it was times like this she felt like she was his mother.

When Rod didn't come to school or come home at night, it always worried her because it left her wondering whether he was OK or not. With the crowd he hung around, she feared she would lose him sooner than his time. There was no way she could go on with her day not knowing where Rod was. So, she went to the office and asked to use the phone. Diamond buzzed Rod's right-hand man, Black. She knew for sure Rod had to be with him because that was his best friend and they stuck together like glue.

"Black, it's Diamond. Is Rod with you?"

"I just left him. He's at the house."

"OK. Thank you."

She was relieved to know he was good, but she was furious about him missing another day of school. Diamond hated when that happened. He was a senior, so close to finishing, and she was hoping that he would hang in there just a little while longer. He would be the first guy in their family to graduate high school, and that was why Diamond was so hard on him about going. Although Rod didn't think much of him getting a piece of paper that said he completed all of his school years, Diamond did. She was all about breaking cycles and making sure they made a better life for themselves than what their parents gave them.

After school was over, she went straight home only to find an eviction notice on the front door. With no emotions, she snatched it off to keep others from seeing and walked inside. She found Rod lying on the couch sleep, with Black and a few other guys near him in the living room, rolling up a blunt, talking and laughing loudly.

Interrupting his sleep she slapped on his leg. "Why didn't you come to school today? You know what, forget that. Look what was on the door again. It's the final notice, Rod! What the hell are we gonna do?" Before he could speak, she crumbled the piece of paper and tossed it at him.

She went into her room to calm herself. She started on her homework to clear her head, but with so much on her mind, she couldn't focus. Tossing her work to the other side of the room, she lay on top of the blanket that was on the floor, staring at the ceiling. Before she knew it, she was waking up from a nap she had no intention of taking. Almost forgetting about the twins, she hopped up to go and get them.

When she got to the kitchen, she saw Rod and his boys surrounding the table with lots of ski masks and guns that covered the tabletop.

"What the fuck is going on?"

"Chill, sis. Everything's good. Do you wanna get put out and be homeless? Do you want to get the twins taken from you and us all go to foster care, waiting around to be adopted by motherfuckers who really don't give a fuck about us? Do you want us to end up living with strangers worse off than our own fuckin' parents?"

"No!"

"OK then. Just let me do what I need to do, and keep your mouth shut about it."

He rounded his boys, all six of them. All he said was, "Come on, y'all. Get right." And from there on, they knew what to do. They each grabbed a ski mask and threw them on their heads. Then they each grabbed a gun off the table and tucked it in their pants.

"Are y'all ready?" Black asked.

"Hell yeah," they replied.

"Let's go get these motherfuckers."

"Wait!" Diamond hollered. She tried talking to Rod before he left, but the door slammed in her face.

With the sun starting to set and still no electricity, Diamond went to pick up the twins from Ms. Mable's like she was going to do before getting sidetracked. She wanted to wash them and put them to bed before it got too dark in the house. When she went over, Ms. Mable welcomed her in.

As Diamond entered, her nose grew wide, and her eyes closed instantly from the whiff she got from the home-cooked meal she wasn't used to smelling. The smell of hot chicken grease and pork and beans with sausage made her stomach growl loudly.

"The twins are in the playpen!" Ms. Mable hollered from the kitchen.

"You know, you can stay for dinner if you'd like."

"I don't know. It's getting late."

"Hmm… A good reason for y'all to stay, isn't it? Ain't like there's light in the place anyways."

"How'd you figure?" Diamond asked. Diamond never mentioned their situation to anyone, not even Ms. Mable, because she was embarrassed about it.

"Ms. Mable knows everything, baby. I've been here a long time, thirty years to be exact. I wasn't always fortunate to pay my light bill. Many times, I had to flick lighters to get through the house and light candles in each room to see. It ain't nothing for you to be ashamed of. Your mother ought to be ashamed of herself for not doing right by y'all. Now at least let me feed the kids. They have not eaten dinner yet."

"OK. I guess… I guess I'll take a plate too."

Ms. Mable looked back and smiled at her as she fixed a plate for all of them.

"I'm going to make a plate for Rodney as well."

"He's not home," Diamond said.

"Where is he?"

"I'm… I'm not sure." Diamond stuttered.

After they ate, Diamond and Ms. Mable talked about the twins and how school was going. They watched TV together, then Diamond quickly fell asleep on the couch with the twins cuddled up next to her. Ms. Mable took the twins from beside her and laid them in the playpen. She threw sheets across each of them and turned out the lights. Before she headed out of the room, she whispered to Diamond. "Ms. Mable knows everything, sweetie."

The next day was Saturday, and with no school for Diamond, Ms. Mable let them sleep as long as they wanted. Once Diamond realized she wasn't home, she hopped up quickly and grabbed the twins to head out. She was hoping Rod would be home by now. She didn't know what happened to him last night when he went to hit the lick.

When she walked in the back door of their apartment, she couldn't help but notice all the money, weed, and jewelry that was on the table. She went to take the twins in the room then went back in the kitchen. She stood next to the table, running her fingers over the jewelry. Diamond was fascinated by how beautiful it was. She wasn't thrilled about what Rod had went and done to get it, but she was overjoyed that soon they would have electricity and food again. She was relieved that the rent would be paid, and they would still have a roof over their heads.

"Before you say anything, just let me—" Rod started to say.

Diamond cut his sentence short and said, "Thank you."

"Whatever you do, don't touch any of this. I'll give you money once I figure this out," Rod told her.

Not too long after Diamond went back in the room to her boys, she called Rod.

She asked him to watch the twins while she ran over to a classmate's house to grab some free clothes her mom was giving to her boys. Without hesitating, Rod agreed to watch the twins for her. On Diamond's way out of the house, she walked past the table again. She saw how much the jewelry shined brightly and glistened from the sunlight that beamed through the windows.

She stopped by the table and touched the diamond necklace she had her eyes on since the first time she came across it. *This is gorgeous; I want this,* she whispered to herself, dangling it in the air, admiring how beautiful it was. She looked down the hall to see if Rod was coming. Since he wasn't, she snatched the necklace along with the matching bracelet and ran out the door.

Diamond waited until she got some distance from the house before throwing them on. She walked through the neighborhood, showing off the stolen material she didn't think much about. Walking with her head held high, she smiled from the compliments she got on it, which she didn't get on a regular basis.

Once she got the clothes, she headed back home like she told Rod she would. Diamond walked in the house, forgetting to take off the jewelry she wasn't supposed to have in the first place. Before she could do so, Rod caught her.

"Didn't I tell you not to touch shit? Take it off!"

"It was pretty. I just wanted to wear it until I came back. Damn! You can have it back. It's not a big deal."

"Yes it is! What if the wrong person saw you with this? What if someone snatched it off you? This is for me to sell! We need the money. Just listen to me!" Rod argued.

"You shouldn't be stealing anyways, if you're that concerned about our safety. Just go and get a real job! You hang with Black and them, for what? Trouble? They don't care about you like I do! We need you here."

"You don't know what you're talking about! You know what, I'm not about to listen to you bicker… I'm out!" Rod said.

Rod walked toward the door. Before Diamond could say anything else, Rod was out like he said he was, leaving the screen door to slam behind him.

Diamond stood in the kitchen, rolling her eyes and shaking her head. She went in the cabinets and ran the faucet, putting her glass underneath. "Why do he run out on arguments? Ugh, that pisses me off!" Diamond said. She grabbed her glass and walked along the hallway to her room where her boys were.

Bang! Bang! Bang! Before she got halfway down the hall, she heard gunshots. At first, she didn't think much of it since they heard it so often. That was until she thought about Rod. It was just moments after he left out the house. She ran out of the door to the porch to see if she could see anything, forgetting about the twins. When she got outside, she saw a young guy lying on the ground in a pool of blood. She instantly dropped her glass, leaving it shattered on the ground in front of the door. The guy who was lying on the ground was Rod.

She ran over to the body like everyone else. Ms. Mable came out of her apartment as well. She tried asking Diamond what was going on, but Diamond was too far gone by then. She saw Diamond didn't have the twins with her, so she walked down to Diamond's place to grab them. When she got there, the twins were crying loudly, but it didn't distract her from all the stolen goods, money, and drugs that lie on their kitchen table.

When Diamond came up to the crowd that surrounded the body, she pushed folks aside to get to him.

"Move! That's my brother! That's my brother!" she hollered.

She dropped to her knees beside Rod in the middle of the street. She lifted his head, resting it on her forearm.

"Noooooo!" She hollered loudly.

"Someone, call 911. Tell them we need an ambulance, now!" a woman said in the back of the crowd.

Diamond shook his body with her other hand. "Rod? I need you to wake up. Open your eyes, please. Come on, open your eyes." Diamond kept shaking him then tried opening his eyes herself.

She rubbed over his chest where he constantly bled, looking at her hand covered with his blood, trying to understand if it was real. She started shaking him again. She kept shaking him as she hollered repeatedly. "Wake up, Rod! I need you! Get up! Just come back! Please! I need you here! Nooooo!"

Chapter 1

"Scared money don't make money"

Diamond tossed and turned in her sleep. She often had nightmares about the day Rod got shot. It had been three years now, but with justice not served, she never found peace.

"Diamond? Diamond! Get up!" Her best friend Naomi hollered. She continuously shook Diamond until she finally woke up.

"You're having another nightmare, again. You've overslept already anyways. You're gonna be late for work."

"Oh shit! What time is it? Lord knows I can't afford to lose this job. Ain't like it pays much anyways, but I still need it."

Diamond often complained to Naomi about not making enough money. Life was rough back in the days with Rod's help, but now that he was gone, it was a true struggle for her. It was so hard, she ended up moving with Naomi in the projects on the East side.

Diamond was desperate for help. She even started searching for her kids' father, but unfortunately, she had no luck with it. He impregnated her when she was fifteen, and he was twenty-three at the time. Right before she gave birth, he found out how old she really was and vanished.

He knew people would label him as a child molester, so he didn't want anything to do with her. It wasn't like he was planning on fathering

14

her kids anyways. At that age, all he was focused on was smoking drugs and selling it.

Diamond became numb to neglect. It was normal for men to do that to women where she came from. Her mother was a single mom as well, and her father didn't give a shit about her or Rod either.

Diamond did the best she could for the three of them but soon got evicted when her five hundred dollars a month income wasn't enough. Diamond was thankful that she was good to Naomi at Burger King because they became really good friends. Naomi became Diamond's backbone and replaced Rod with the help she received. Naomi opened her doors to Diamond and her boys. Ms. Mable offered her a place to stay as well, but Diamond damn sure didn't want to move in with her and put up with all her rules. As a young girl, she wanted to be comfortable where she stayed, and with Naomi just a year older than her, she knew she could be wild and free at Naomi's if she wanted to. At Ms. Mable's, it was a different story. That kind of behavior would never fly.

Naomi was more like a sister to Diamond, and she treated the twins like her own. Naomi didn't have kids but wanted them. Before she broke up with her long-time boyfriend of four years, she tried getting pregnant but never did. During their relationship, she found out she couldn't have kids, possibly due to her being molested many times by her uncle when she was a kid. When she told her boyfriend the news, he was devasted. After he found out, he left her and got another girl pregnant. Naomi broke up with him afterwards and never went back. That happened before her and Diamond met, but when her and Diamond got close and mentioned her raising the twins on her own, Naomi offered to help.

Naomi was so good with kids. She watched after them, fed them, bought them toys, shoes, and clothes when she had it, played with them, and even whipped their asses when they got into shit they weren't supposed to. Naomi was more like their second mom, and Diamond didn't trip; she needed all the help she could get with them.

Naomi sat on Diamond's bedroom floor while Diamond got ready for work.

"You're always complaining about going to work. I don't understand why you wanna stay at Burger King anyways. You don't make any money there. What you need to do is come on down to the club and make some real money."

"I've told you already, that ain't me. I'm not trying to judge, but I'm not the type of chick to go out there and shake my ass for dollars… I'm too shy for that shit."

"Scared money don't make money. With all that ass you got, you're bound to bring home at least a band a night. I'll teach you what you need to know, and I'll be there with you every night. A big party is going on this Saturday, and they are still looking for more dancers. All you have to do is say the word, and I'll holla at Red Man for you."

"This Saturday? Like in four days Saturday?"

"Yeah!"

"I don't know. That's so soon."

"Ain't like you don't need money right now. What are you waiting for?"

"Listen, I gotta go. Let's talk about this some other time," Diamond told her.

Before she headed out, she went over to the boys and kneeled beside them. She held them tightly then slobbered all over their cheeks. They wiped their cheeks with the back of their hands as soon as Diamond turned them loose.

"Eww, Ma! We are not babies anymore," Josh said.

"Y'all will always be mama babies," she told them, just before snatching her keys off the coffee table and running out the door.

She went outside and got in her car. *Tick, Tick, Tick, Tick* was the noise she heard the car make as she tried starting it, which turned out to be an epic fail because the ignition just rattled. The car was no good, and she knew it. It often gave her trouble, and it didn't fail her this time either. It wasn't much she could do about it when she barely had enough money to put food on the table. She fought with it each time until it decided to work properly. She turned the key back to try it again. *Tick, Tick, Tick, Tick.* The sound repeated.

"Damn! I'm tired of this piece of shit ass car!" she yelled.

She didn't have time to fight with it, so she got out of the car and went back in the house, hollering to Naomi.

"I need to borrow your car. Please," she begged.

"Yo' shit ain't working again today?"

"Hell no, and I'm already late. I don't have time to play with it today. The bus will take too long, and I don't have enough money to catch a cab. I get my check today. I'll put gas in your car before I return it."

Naomi handed over her keys to Diamond. "Make sure you're back in time. I have to go to the club tonight."

"I will; no worries," Diamond told her.

When Diamond got to work, her manager told her that she wasn't needed today and that they tried calling her, but her line was disconnected.

"Ms. Lorraine, I need this shift. I can't miss out on any money. I need all that I can get. Besides, I'm already here. Is there anything else I can do around here?"

"I'm sorry, Diamond. It's been pretty slow today. We've been sending people home all morning. We have all the people we need already."

Diamond was frustrated and worried about how much those few hours would make a tremendous difference on her check. Diamond slapped the wall in anger, and Ms. Lorraine stood in Diamond's shadow, watching her. Diamond was always one of the quiet ones, so she couldn't believe her behavior. Ms. Lorraine stood silently with her hands on her hips and lips scrunched, watching Diamond.

"Shit! Well, can I at least get my check?" Diamond asked her.

Without saying a word, she led Diamond into the office. She handed her the check, and Diamond headed out the door. She waited until she got in the car to tear open the envelope, only to find herself angrier after doing so.

"Two hundred and twenty-five dollars?"

She was pissed about how small her check was after busting her ass doing ten hours of overtime. She was expecting to have more so she could get her car fixed, phone turned back on, and have a decent amount to spend the night of her 21st birthday, but with the check she had, she wasn't sure if that would be possible.

Working at Burger King making $7.25 an hour with occasional overtime barely helped her make ends meet. She was tired of living paycheck to paycheck and not being able to do the things for her and her kids that she wanted. Like put them in their own place, drive a decent car that worked all the time and not just when it felt like it, and buy her kids new shoes and clothes, instead of shopping at the Goodwill for hand me downs.

She started to consider the offer Naomi made her about working at the club, even though she was still uncomfortable about it and considerably shy. When she headed back to the house, Naomi and the twins weren't expecting to see her back so soon.

"Damn, what happened? You got fired, didn't you?"

"No. They sent me home. She said they were slow today and didn't need me. I need my fuckin' money. Now, my next check will be short like it ain't already, when I am working all my hours."

"That job is full of shit. That's why I left. They have their people picked. You buss your ass there. They should have sent one of those lazy bitches home who likes to stand around and take snapchat pics, instead of you. Fuck that job, sis. C'mon. Shake all that ass you got at the club. You could make a killer. I'm telling you. Saturday is gonna be epic. The place is supposed to be packed. Everybody's talking about it. I even heard all the ballin' niggas are supposed to be there. They always roll deep and throw lots of cash. I'm talking about at least a few hundred dollars each. I'm trying to come home with at least three grand. Take the kids to Ms. Mable's; she wouldn't mind. You won't regret this shit. I'm tellin' you. Just think about it."

"Yeah, I will because this check ain't gon' cut it. What the fuck am I supposed to do with two hundred dollars?" Diamond said, waving the paper check she held in her hand.

Diamond never clubbed, let alone twerked. She didn't know the first thing about dancing or even knew what the inside of a strip club looked like. Dancing was never her thing, and she never had interest in hanging out at a strip club either. All she knew was what she saw on TV and what Naomi told her.

Naomi knew Diamond was a bad ass bitch and not because that was her friend. Diamond was a pretty faced, thick chick that stood at five feet eight inches with fairly long legs. She knew that Diamond could make good money and hated for her to pass up the opportunity. There was no way she could take no for an answer from her.

All night while Naomi was out working, Diamond thought about if she should try it out or not. She was so worried about being judged and the thoughts other people would have of her, that she wasn't looking at the bigger picture and truly understanding how much of a life changing opportunity it was. That was until she realized she didn't have a choice.

She went in the living room and went on YouTube, and once the kids went to sleep, she searched for twerk videos. She snuck inside of Naomi's room and went into her closet, shuffling through many pairs of flats and sneakers in order for her to get to Naomi's heels she often wore to the club. She tried on many to see which ones she was most comfortable in.

When she found the pair that she liked, she threw them on and started practicing in the mirror. She went at it for hours. It was much harder for her than what the girls on YouTube made it seem. The only thing Diamond knew how to do already was a full split, which was a plus for starters. When it came to twerking and understanding the concept, she sucked. She was an amateur with no rhythm.

Diamond stood in the mirror and turned slightly to the side, looking at herself squeeze on her perfectly plump ass, moving it up and down with her hands. "It's a shame I have all of this and don't know how to use it."

This chick had the body of a goddess. She didn't have much boobs, wearing a C cup, but when it came to her hips, oh baby, her waist was slim with the ass that females paid thousands for these days. Her body was banging, leaving everyone with no idea that she carried two kids at the same time. The girl didn't have an inch of fat on her body. The only thing that could be said was the chick was blessed.

Diamond followed along with the videos and danced nonstop, but she couldn't seem to get the hang of it like them. Just when she was getting ready to quit, she started to make progress.

"OK! I'm finally getting somewhere," she told herself.

"Yes, you are! Your moves aren't perfect, but you'll get there. Just keep practicing; you're doing great," she heard Naomi say. Diamond jumped up, stumbling in the five-inch heels, as her heart pounded rapidly in her chest.

"Oh shit! You scared me," she told Naomi, gasping for air, trying her hardest to catch her breath. "How long have you been standing there?"

"Long enough," Naomi told her as she came into the room and tossed her duffel bag on the bed. Then she went toward her Bluetooth speaker on the dresser. She went through her phone, and shortly after, R. Kelly's "Bump and Grind" song came on. Naomi sat at the edge of her bed and grabbed her favorite heels out of her duffel bag. She slid them on and stood in front of the mirror next to Diamond.

"This is a classic right here. They play this in the club all the time. If you can groove to this, you can groove to anything. When you dance, you gotta get into it. Make them motherfuckers feel you. Make them wanna spend their money on you instead of those other bitches.

You can be friends with them, but when we are on stage, it's a competition. The sexier you look, the more tricks you do, the more ass you make clap, the more money you will make. It's that simple."

Naomi turned the music up and threw her phone on the bed. She started winding her body slowly from side to side like a slithering snake as she made love to the mirror. She ran her long fingernails along her body as she threw a finger from her other hand in her mouth and closed her teeth slightly on it. She wrapped an arm around her neck and rubbed across it slowly to the beat. Bent halfway over with her back arched deeply, she made her ass wiggle.

Before Diamond's eyes, Naomi dropped down to the floor in a split. Diamond watched Naomi as she quickly turned and flipped her leg over the other then ended on her knees, bouncing each of her ass cheeks to R. Kelly's voice. Diamond could tell when she was on stage, she worked her ass off to get paid what she knew she deserved.

Diamond had seen her dancing around the house before, and she knew she had moves, but Diamond had no idea she was as good as she was. Naomi only showed Diamond a sample, but it left her amazed. She was dying to learn what Naomi knew how to do.

Naomi got up off the floor and turned off the music.

"It's not all about twerking at a strip club. You have to learn how to dance passionately to slow music as well. That's just a little bit of what I do. You need to see me on a pole."

"I don't have to. From what you just did, I know you are probably the best. I wanna learn."

"So, you have decided to come to the club?"

"I don't know if I'll be ready in four days. I have a lot to learn by then."

"I'm willing to teach you if you're serious about this."

Diamond was still indecisive about if she wanted to go or not. That was until she saw what Naomi had. Naomi went in her duffel bag and pulled out two stacks that amounted to a hundred each.

"Damn, you made this all in one night?"

Naomi looked at Diamond with a smirk. She reached in her duffel bag and pulled three more stacks that amounted to three hundred total. Diamond's eyes grew wide. She didn't know that amount of money could be made so quickly.

"This has to be around a grand," Diamond said to her.

"It looks like more than what it is because it's lots of ones, but it's not quite that much. Each stack is a hundred dollars."

"One, two, three, four, five hundred dollars? You made all of this in three hours? That's more than I make in two weeks. Geesh!"

"Yeah, and it's only Tuesday. So just imagine what I'm bringing home on Saturday and how much you could too. Have you made your mind up yet?"

"I'll have to find a way to get over my fears. I need this money!" Diamond told her.

Naomi smiled. "Say no more. I got you!"

Diamond got up to return Naomi's heels back to her closet. She went to her room and closed the door behind her. She stood with her back against it, throwing her hands on her head and giving it a slight squeeze. She couldn't believe what she'd told Naomi. She wasn't ready; she knew she wasn't. She still didn't know how to dance, and the thought of her climbing a pole scared the hell out of her.

"What the fuck did I just do?" She whispered to herself.

Chapter 2

"Go and Get It"

Diamond was off for the next couple of days, so she decided to hang with Naomi the next day to get prepared for Saturday at the club. Naomi took Diamond to drop the kids off to Ms. Mable's until they were done.

She left the twins and Ms. Mable with the impression that she was going to her job at Burger King, never mentioning to them that she was starting a new job at the strip club. She sat in the passenger seat of Naomi's car, clueless to where she was being taken. Soon, they pulled up to a building that read *Exotic Dance Studio and Gear*.

"I can't go inside there in front of all those women and I don't know what I am doing."

"Diamond, calm down. One of my good friends owns this studio. I got us a private session with her, so don't worry. You said last night that you wanted to learn what I know, and this is how I know what to do. Just chill. She's a cool chick. You can learn a lot from her."

"Damn, can't we just go back to the house so I can practice in the mirror a little bit more?"

"YouTube and practicing in the mirror aren't going to get you the moves that you need in this short period of time. We only have three days left, Diamond. Do you want this money or not?"

Diamond looked in the back seat and snatched a pair of heels. It was a good thing that her and Naomi wore the same size; otherwise, she would be screwed. She got out of the car and stood on the sidewalk with her arms crossed, waiting for Naomi to get out the car and lead her in. When Naomi got out of the car, she laughed at how much Diamond was acting like a kid and pouting as if she wasn't turning twenty-one in just two days. Naomi grabbed her by the hand. "Come on, girl. You got this; you will be fine."

When Diamond walked in the studio and saw for herself that no one else was in the room except them, she became more comfortable about dancing, but while she waited for Joyce to get things in order for them, she started downing herself again.

"Naomi, I can't do this."

Naomi's friend who owned the studio was Joyce. Joyce walked over to Diamond and Naomi after overhearing what Diamond said.

"It's OK, beautiful. It's normal to feel this way when you have never done this before. A lot of women walk in here not confident and unsure, but when they leave, they thank me for giving them a good experience, and they come back again and again. By the time you leave here today, I promise you will feel so much better. Don't be too hard on yourself. Don't think too much about it; just loosen up, live in the moment, and have fun."

"Naomi, take her to the more exciting side of the building. I'm sure she will loosen up after seeing that," Joyce continued.

Naomi grabbed Diamond and took her to the store on the other side of the building to pick out some outfits and gear. She wanted it to resemble what it would be like on the stage as much as possible so Diamond wouldn't be scared or surprised when the time came.

She knew Diamond's favorite color was red and pink, so she showed her a few pieces in those colors. Diamond showed interest in a few outfits, but she really loved the hot pink one. It was a stretchy high waist two piece with a thong back. She picked out some pretty glittered six-inch platform heels to start with. Once Diamond went to try everything on and saw herself in the mirror, she got excited.

"Damn, I'm a bad bitch," she said, twirling and admiring how sexy she looked.

"That's what I'm talking about! Now you look like you're ready. C'mon, let's hit these poles and have some fun," Naomi said.

Joyce started them off with booty tricks and twerk. They did that for an hour as she worked closely with Diamond to make sure she was as close to perfect as she could be. Then she taught Diamond lap and chair dancing. Joyce taught her how to gain more control of her hips, work them properly, and shake her ass good enough so that she could bring home a hefty amount of money. The last yet hardest thing for Diamond to do was work the pole.

Diamond's upper body strength sucked, which was to be expected as such an amateur. She could climb, but constantly doing it tired her. Although it wasn't easy, she never gave up. She wanted that money—she was determined to get it—so she made sure she gave it her all to master it.

"You're doing great, Diamond. Remember, just because you are a stripper doesn't mean you have to climb poles. If you aren't comfortable with doing it Saturday, then don't. I'd rather you not do it than to make a fool of yourself," Joyce told her.

Naomi knew how long it would take her to get it down. She'd been stripping for two years now, and she still wasn't perfect at what she did. She still took classes. When she saw what Diamond could do by the end of the class, she was impressed. She knew she would need more work but was ready to take on Saturday night.

When Diamond and Naomi left the studio, Naomi took Diamond to get a nice wig and to get their manicures and pedicures, where they took the time to talk.

"I never knew what made you do this, so tell me, why?"

"What? Pay for all of this?" Naomi asked.

"No, work at the club."

"Listen, I was in the same boat as you. I was living with my grandma. I wasn't making any money at Burger King either, and that's when I left. When I left, I had no plan B. I didn't have anyone to help me get another job that paid decent either. After about a month of sitting at home, I rode past the club. I stopped and went in, and that's when I fell in love with it. I've always loved dancing. I took classes as a kid, not knowing that I would end up at a strip club, but it paid the bills."

"I didn't know you would get that deep. I didn't mean to put your business out in here."

Naomi was never ashamed of being a stripper, so she talked about it freely. She never cared about what people thought. She loved what she did, and she would let the world know it, every chance she got.

Naomi shrugged. "It's not a big deal. I don't care."

"How much longer are you going to do this?" Diamond asked.

"Just until I get enough money to open up my hair salon. It was never a dream of mine to be naked in front of strange ass men, who didn't get pussy at home and came to the club to fulfill their fantasies. I'm still there because I know how much money I can make. When I get the money that I need, I'm getting the hell out the hood, getting a nice place, and leaving this stripping shit behind me."

"Damn! You do make really good money there. I'm sure you'll be out of there before you know it."

"Yeah, hopefully."

"I wonder how long it'll be before I'm able to walk away from it too," Diamond said.

"The most important thing to remember is not to get sucked in too deep. A lot of women see the money and never wanna leave. Don't be that bitch. Focus on your reason for being there. Do it while you have to, make a plan to get you out of it, and stick to it so you never have to go back," Naomi told her.

"Enough about this. Are you excited about your birthday? Girl, you're about to be able to drink legally now. Twenty-one is a big fuckin' deal."

"Yeah, I am, but not excited as I should be. My check fucked that up for me."

"Listen, quit actin' like I ain't got you. We gon' have fun! Have you decided on where we are going?"

"I think we should go downtown and party with the white folks. They know how to have fun without fussing, fighting, and shooting. I'm getting older. I don't want that ratchet shit around me," Diamond explained.

When they were done at the nail salon, they went to get the boys. Diamond practiced more when she got home, implementing what she learned from Joyce.

"Mommy? What are you doing?" Jordan asked Diamond. She immediately stopped what she was doing because she never wanted her boys to see her dancing like that in the first place.

"She's dancing, duh," Josh told him.

"Be nice, Joshua. I need to talk to the both of you for a second. Come sit down by me."

Diamond continued. "Mommy has a new job now, and it's a little different from the job I had. Well, a lot different."

"What kind of job is it?" Josh asked.

Diamond sat quietly as she thought about the best way to answer her five-year-old's question.

"It's just different. I will be home more in the day, but y'all won't see me much at night. Y'all will spend more time at Ms. Mable's, but I'll still be able to take y'all to school in the mornings. Auntie MiMi and I will be working together, so I will be fine."

"So does that mean we won't get any more burgers?" Jordan asked.

Diamond laughed because, for a second, she forgot about the things kids asked and how funny they were.

"My new job doesn't sell burgers, but I'll be making more money, so I can buy y'all burgers from wherever y'all like. Burger King burgers weren't all that good anyways."

They all laughed. She grabbed the twins and set them each on her legs. She hugged and kissed them on the foreheads.

"And you wanna know what else? I'll be able to get my car fixed, get us into our own place, and make sure y'all get your own rooms. I'll be able to take y'all to the mall to get new clothes and shoes. I might even let y'all shop until y'all drop. How does that sound?"

"Great!" the twins said excitedly.

She sent them off to bed since school was in the morning. She continued to practice in the room, and that's what she did until she went to bed. She wanted to be able to do more than anyone would expect to see from a newbie on stage. With Saturday being just three days away, practicing made her a little more comfortable and excited about it approaching.

The next day, Diamond walked the twins to school. On her way home, she stopped by Ms. Mable's and knocked on her door.

"Hey, Ms. Mable. Is it fine that I come in? I know I'm here unannounced."

"It's OK. I'm just doing the usual with a house full of bad ass kids, but come on in. Is everything OK? You hardly come by without the boys."

She was shocked to see Diamond alone because, normally, she was dropping the boys off for her to babysit, but it wasn't an issue because she always enjoyed Diamond's company.

"Everything's fine. I wanted to come talk to you."

"What's going on, Diamond?"

"I wanted to come by and check on you. Also to tell you how much I really appreciate all the help you've given us over the years. Things have been rough since Rod died, and I'm still not over it. I don't think I will ever be. Ever since my mom went downhill, you were like a mother to us. Still to this day, I don't know where the hell... I'm sorry. I don't know where she is, but I want to thank you for being here. You are truly a blessing to us."

Ms. Mable wiped her eyes as she walked over to Diamond to hug her. Ms. Mable often got emotional when she heard things like that. Many people came to her for their needs, and she always helped without hesitating, but not many showed or even told her how thankful they were for what she did for them.

"Listen, baby. I know that you appreciate me, that's why I've stuck around and helped you. Rod was all you had, and once you lost him, I was praying for you. I was worried about you and the boys. God gave you Naomi to help heal you, but I'll always be here for y'all as long as I live. I don't know how much longer it will be though."

"Oh, Ms. Mable, don't talk like that. Is there something wrong? Have you been taking care of yourself?"

"As much as I can, baby, but this lupus has been causing lots of complications. It's not easy, but I'll be OK. Don't you worry about me."

"Oh, Ms. Mable! All this time, and I never knew."

"It's because I don't want you to worry."

I know I don't have much to offer, but I'm here for you if you need me. I don't have much money right now, but I know how to cook and clean. I can lend you a hand or two, and when I get some money, I want to look out for you as well."

"Didn't I tell you not to worry about me. Just take care of yourself and my boys. I'll be fine... really!"

"I'm hoping to have some good money soon. I'm starting a new night job that should pay me well."

"Oh, baby, that's good! I'm proud of you! Congratulations."

Diamond didn't want to mention to Ms. Mable where her job was or what she was doing. She knew Ms. Mable wouldn't approve of it and would give her a lecture about it. She knew it wasn't the best thing for her to be doing, and she didn't want to hear about it. Diamond was still iffy about going, but after all the preparation she did, she didn't want anything or anyone to change her mind about it.

"Thank you. I'm excited about it. I would need to bring the boys around eight p.m. every night I work. I'll come by early in the morning to get them ready for school and keep them on the weekends when I don't work."

"Well, what kind of job is it? You ain't out there selling your body for money, now are you?"

"No ma'am. I'm not prostituting. It's at the club, bartending." Diamond lied.

"Oh yeah. I heard bartenders make pretty good money, especially from the tips all of those drunk ass men give."

Diamond laughed. "Yeah, those tips are where the money really comes from."

"Well you just be safe in that club. People can get crazy as hell after they drink. I'll be happy to keep the boys for you. You are lucky they are pretty good kids. If they weren't well mannered and behaved, you would be on your own."

"I appreciate this. One last thing, my birthday is tomorrow night, and I want to go out with my friend for fun. I know I'm not working, but can I still bring them by?"

"Uhhh… why not?" Ms. Mable said.

Diamond grabbed Ms. Mable and squeezed her tight as she repeatedly thanked her.

"I'm going to leave now. I need to take care of some things before it's time for them to get out of school."

Diamond left Ms. Mable's house and walked home thinking about how much she'd been through. Often times she thought about her mother and wondered if she was dead or alive. She wondered if her mother cared or thought about them. She never showed up to Rod's service and that angered her.

She thought about how life would have been if Rod was still here. She blamed herself for his death. She felt like if they never argued, he never would have died. Diamond was living in anger and regret. She would always put the burden of his death on herself, when the demons who killed him should have been the ones wearing it.

After Rod died, his homeboys vanished. Diamond never saw them again. She believed they were the ones that came back in the house and took back all that they had stolen, but she had no proof. They were close to Rod, and she thought they would have offered her money or even help, but they didn't. She knew they weren't his real friends, and that was why she stressed to him about parting ways with them, but he was too hardheaded to listen to what she told him.

Even though Rod got killed in broad daylight, nobody seemed to have witnessed the shooting. Everybody kept quiet, and because of that, the cops still didn't have a suspect in custody. They stuck to the no snitching rules the streets held. He was another black man lost to gun violence, with an unsolved case that the cops didn't care about.

When Diamond finally got in the house, Naomi was in the kitchen making herself some breakfast.

"What took you so long? I was worried something happened to you, girl."

Diamond laughed. "No. I stopped by Ms. Mable's and talked to her about watching the boys at night instead of during the day."

"What did her nosy ass say?"

"She was fine with it. Ms. Mable isn't a bad person. I love that woman, actually."

"She is a bitch, Diamond. Let's be honest."

"She's not. She wants the best for everyone and always willing to help out if she can. You were rude the very first time you met her.

She told you off like any old lady would. That doesn't make her a bitch, Naomi."

Naomi laughed. "I guess you're right, but she's still mean. So, anyways, how are you feeling now that Saturday is two days away?"

"I'm excited about it actually. I want to make money, but I'm also going to have some fun with it, just like Joyce said. I haven't drunk in a while, so I'm going to throw a few shots back and give it a try. I hate that my first night is going to be on such a busy one though. I wish I was able to work a slow day and get a feel for it first."

"I don't think a slow day would make things any better, because not many people would be there. I know when I'm dancing on a slow night, I get pissed. I get pissed that I'm working my ass off and not making much of anything. Just because not many people are there doesn't mean that you can slack on your dancing. You would still have to give it your all because that's your reputation. Once you fuck up one night and they come back another, they may not fuck with you anymore. All because of that one slow night you slacked. Moral of the story, give it your all, no matter how much money you make."

"I guess I didn't think about it like that," Diamond replied.

.

Chapter 3

"Pop that Pussy"

It was finally Friday, the day Diamond had been waiting on so she could unwind and have fun. After spending time with the boys once they got from school, she took them to Ms. Mable's. When she got back to the house, MiMi was in the bathroom listening to Kevin Gates while she got dressed.

"Biiiiiitch! It's your birthday! Are you ready for tonight?" Naomi hollered to Diamond after realizing she was back.

"Yessss! I'm ready!" She hollered back as she threw her hands in the air and pretended to twerk.

"Hold up, wait. I have the perfect song for you," Naomi said as she walked out of the bathroom into her room where her phone was. Moments later, Uncle Luke's "It's your Birthday" song came on.

Naomi hyped Diamond up after Diamond told her how she wasn't excited much about her birthday. Naomi was always the life of the party and knew how to have fun, even when she was down. Naomi was just the person Diamond needed around tonight.

"Come on, Dime. Let's get it," Naomi told her as she bounced with every step she took, walking toward Diamond.

"Go, Diamond. It's your birthday!" Naomi sung while she twerked.

What Diamond didn't know was that Naomi already had been sipping on some Amsterdam and pineapple juice, so she was ready to turn up and make the night memorable.

Naomi continued to sing. "Come on, Diamond, it's your birthday!"

Diamond threw her hands on her knees and arched her back as she started shaking her ass to the music. Naomi came closer to Diamond and watched her. Naomi threw one hand in the air and hollered, "Aye, get it, get it! Bitch, you better work it," while she slapped on Diamond's ass. They weren't bisexual by any means, but often times they did things like that to hype the next person or to make the moment more enjoyable.

Diamond stuck her tongue out while she smiled and kept dancing for a few minutes longer. Before the song was over, Diamond called it quits, and the girls started laughing.

"Bitch, you was getting it!" Naomi told her.

"I can do a little something," Diamond joked.

Diamond continued. "I can't be foolin' up wit' you. If I keep going, we will never make it out of here."

Naomi agreed. "You're right." She turned Kevin Gates back on and went back in the bathroom to finish her makeup. Diamond washed and threw on a cute fuchsia pink, strapless bodycon dress and some white pumps. With how drunk she had planned on getting, she didn't bother bringing a clutch or purse with her because she knew she would lose it. Instead, she stuffed everything in the strapless bra she wore.

As she waited for Naomi to do her makeup, she threw on her blonde wig and moisturized with body oil with a dash of body glitter on her chest. After Naomi finally did Diamond's makeup, their Uber arrived at 10:30 p.m.

When they got there, the lines were long as hell. While they waited, they laughed and talked. Right before they went inside, Naomi pointed out Diamond's wig.

"I see you have the blonde one on tonight."

Diamond patted her head, forgetting which wig she pulled out. "Well, they say blondes have more fun. Let's see if that's true or not," she joked.

When they finally got in, the place was jam packed and lit. They knew they would have a good time for sure. As soon as they got to the bar and ordered their shots of tequila, two white dudes came up on each side of them. They knew how much fun they could have with them and how much money they could save keeping them around for the night, so they did.

They took shots with the guys then went on the dance floor with them. After Diamond told the guy tonight was her 21st birthday, he bought her drinks the rest of the night. By the time Diamond and Naomi left, the guys had them white girl wasted. They stumbled as they walked, bumping into everyone as they exited the club.

Diamond and Naomi walked along the sideway with their arms wrapped around each other, trying to remember where the car was that they never drove. They were so drunk, they forgot how they got to the club.

"Where the hell is the car?" Naomi asked.

"Who cares. It's my fucking birthday!" Diamond yelled loudly, not caring who looked at them crazy.

Naomi stopped on the sidewalk and looked around. "Hold up, we didn't drive here. We caught an Uber. Damn! How did we forget that?"

"We're drunk. We are fucked up, MiMi!"

"I think it's time we get the Uber," Naomi said.

"Yeah… get the fuckin' Uber," Diamond's drunk ass replied.

When they woke up the next morning, they laid in bed all day, trying to recover from the bad hangover they had.

"Ugh, what am I gonna do about this? It's already three p.m., and I'm just getting up. How am I gonna function and get right by tonight?" Diamond said, rubbing her hands across her face.

"I don't know. I don't think I've ever drink that much. Back to back, that guy was like, 'come on, let's go get another drink.' Shit it was free, so I followed him. Now look at me, all helpless n' shit," Naomi said.

They laughed. "Listen, I had a good ass time, even though I feel terrible now."

"That's all that matters," Naomi told her.

Diamond got up to go to the bathroom then turned around in Naomi's direction.

"Oh, and by the way, blondes do have more fun."

***

When they got to the club that night, Diamond was completely lost and confused about how things were done.

"Why does it feel like we are sneaking in here?" Diamond whispered to Naomi as they entered through the side door.

"This is what we are supposed to do," Naomi replied.

Diamond didn't have a clue to what was going on, but she followed Naomi's lead. When they got in, Naomi led her to their locker room where all the other women were and set Diamond down.

"I've talked to you a lot about the club and these girls. Don't forget what I told you."

"I won't."

"Another thing, none of us go by our real names. You know me as Naomi, but everybody else calls me Pebbles here. What's your stage name gonna be?"

Diamond didn't know what to say. She hadn't thought much about that, so she came up with something quickly.

"I guess I'll go by Dream."

Naomi got up and dragged Diamond along. She introduced all the girls to Diamond as Dream. Naomi let them know that Diamond was her girl and she'd be working there now. Some were friendly, but there were others that weren't, who didn't care to introduce themselves or get to know her. When Diamond and Naomi left from by them, Diamond mentioned it to Naomi.

"What's up with the chicks that stood in the back?"

"Remember when I told you it's a competition on stage? Yeah, well, they aren't pleased when new faces come in because they think they will bring less money since there's more people. And I'm not saying it's not possible. Some of these bitches is money hungry and want to leave with all that is thrown. Don't worry about them. They should be the least of your worries. Go out there, have fun like Joyce told you, and make this money."

"I'm ready to get paid!" Diamond replied.

"Now get dressed," Naomi told her.

Diamond and Naomi took care of their hair and makeup before they left the house. All that was needed was for them to get drunk and get dressed. Diamond wore a red short and sexy cup-less striped fishnet chemise, showing off her titties that sat nicely on their own. Underneath, she wore a red G-string with six-inch glass stiletto styled heels.

After they got dressed, Naomi went to her locker where she often hid liquor. She wasn't supposed to have it, but she damn sure wasn't down to spend all her earnings from the club on Red Man's expensive ass bar, so her and Diamond both took three shots of Crown each to start with. Naomi tried not to get Diamond drunk but have her feeling good enough so she wouldn't be so uptight when it was time to go out.

"You know I'm a vodka kind of chick. Why in the hell would you give me brown liquor?"

"Because, it will get you just right. And besides, it's all I have right now. Are you feeling it yet?"

"Hell yeah!"

Shortly after they threw back the alcohol, Red Man came in their locker room and told them they had five minutes before it was time for them to go out. Naomi held Diamond's hand as they bowed their heads and said a prayer. In the little bit of time they had left, they double checked themselves in the mirrors and lined up to head out. When they all heard the deejay calling for the them, they ran from the back and hit the stage. It was showtime.

On the weekends, the deejay started the girls off with something fast and played Uncle Luke's "Doo Doo Brown" song to hype the girls along with the crowd. As the girls ran out and scattered across the stage, Diamond stood there like a deer in front of headlights. She was fascinated by how the club looked. She couldn't believe her first time seeing the inside of a strip club was from her being on stage. So much was going on around her that she couldn't ignore.

The club was lit, literally, with beautiful bright colored lights shining everywhere from the huge disco balls that dangled above their heads. She felt the rhythm of the music in her chest from the loudspeakers that surrounded the club. She stood high, alongside the other dancers who were swinging and climbing the poles. She watched the bottle girls make their way through the crowd to deliver bottles to VIP's. She couldn't believe where she was at this very moment. It felt more like a dream.

Naomi noticed how crazy Diamond looked standing on the stage, so she bumped her on the side. Diamond quickly snapped into reality after being bumped, and the Crown Royal started to kick in more. Diamond started feeling the vibe. She went closer to the edge of the stage.

She started winding her body, similar to what she saw Naomi do. Then she turned around with her bottom facing the crowd. She began bouncing her ass cheeks then made them clap continuously around her G-string without fucking up once. The men in front of her started cheering her on. The way Diamond was moving, nobody could tell she was a rookie to all of it.

She dropped down into a complete split and started bouncing each cheek, one at a time, alternating between the two. She saw the love they were showing her and kept on going. She got back up, bent her knees, and started rolling her hips side to side in rotation of the beat. Right before her eyes, money was raining down on her. Once she saw that, it pumped her up more.

She got off stage and went over to the guys that hyped her up. She stood in front of each of them and shook her ass like her life depended on it. They even grabbed on her, but after Diamond saw the money they were giving, she didn't bother tripping. When they sat down, she bent over to touch her toes without bending a knee. She showed off her smooth, pretty pussy that looked far from the pussy on the stage that was hanging from being ran through, which made them want more from her.

Diamond was having a good time and so was the crowd that watched her. Before it was time for a break, Diamond took a chance at the pole. When she got on it, she worked it like a fucking pro. She owned the stage. She showed the other ladies that she didn't come to play, making the unfriendly chicks madder. She showed the crowd that she wanted all the money and was willing to work for it. Before she knew it, there were, ones, fives, tens, and twenties surrounding her.

She was doing so good, the deejay called her out on the mic. "Alright y'all, there's a new face on the stage, and she goes by Dream. Y'all check her out. She's workin' it. She has a lot of asssss, so spend a lot of cashhhh! C'mon now, don't be cheap!"

The regulars were dying to know who this new chick was that was making the old ones look bad. She was so gone off her liquor and into the moment that she had loosened up completely.

During the break, they all gathered their money and headed in the back. Diamond and Naomi locked up what they had made already and went back out. Naomi walked in front of Diamond as she followed behind. When they were headed back on stage, a guy grabbed Diamond's arm, and Diamond grabbed Naomi's. It was one of the dudes from the crowd that she shook her ass in front of.

"Hey, babe. I saw you on the stage, and damn girl, you a fuckin' beast. You fine as hell too. So, you go by Dream, huh?"

"Yeah, what's up?" Diamond asked.

The guy walked around Diamond, checking out her body, but Diamond stood there about her business, not showing any interest in him. Naomi stood beside Diamond as she listened and watched how Diamond handled herself, ready to hop in if need be. She knew how most of the men tried taking advantage of the new girls, but she was gonna make sure with Diamond, that wasn't the case.

The guy pulled out a stack of money. He took his rubber band from it and started flipping through it. "I'm trying to get a private dance, baby girl. What'd you say?"

"Money talk, bullshit walk. Why you ain't say that a long time ago? Under one condition though."

The guy stopped and looked at Diamond.

"My girl has to come with me. Grab one of your niggas who ain't lacking money and will spend on her."

The guy walked off and went to whisper in one of his homeboy's ear. They sat in VIP with bottles and blunts rolling. Diamond and Naomi knew they had it, and they were on a mission to get it. The guys looked in Diamond and Naomi's direction while they talked. They both walked back over to Diamond and Naomi, and the guy said, "I got one right here for her."

Diamond and Naomi looked at each other, then they led them in the back to a private room that they shared. Although there were security guards that stood outside of the room who checked in periodically, Diamond felt much more comfortable with Naomi by her side.

The guys paid them first, giving each of them a stack of twenties. Once they got the money, they tucked it in their garters and went to work. It was Diamond's first private dance, so she didn't know much about what to do and the limitations she had. She glanced over at Naomi and followed her, but as Diamond ground on him and felt his dick getting rock hard, she started doing tricks of her own. She did whatever until she was told otherwise.

After she ground on him and slid her pussy across his lap many times, she eased her hands in his pants and rubbed on him for a little bit. She kissed on his neck and caressed his chest with her slightly sweaty palms. He was a fine-looking guy; she couldn't deny it. He looked damn good to someone who hadn't gotten laid in over four years. After she felt how hard his dick got and how much of it he had, she wanted to try him. She knew she was there for the money and wasn't supposed to get tied up in other shit, so she didn't make a move on him.

When they were done, Diamond got up off him and left him rock hard. With a tempting body like his, she couldn't believe she did such a thing without getting more from him. She wanted him badly.

Because he had money, he was expecting Diamond to give him a piece of pussy right then and there, but he left disappointed. There was no doubt that he was feeling Diamond and wanted more of her. She was horny from all of it too, but she wasn't down for fucking a nigga she'd never seen before.

As her and Naomi walked off, she felt a touch on her arm, and she turned around. "Dream... wait," he said to her.

"My name is Trill. You are a damn good dancer. You did me right," he said, looking down at his dick as he rubbed on it. She looked down too, trying to stay focused on the bigger picture, although she wanted to try him. "Leave with me tonight. Your girl can come too."

"Hell no! We ain't no fuckin' prostitutes. If y'all are serious about wanting to spend time with us, come to the club. We will be here every Saturday night." Naomi chimed in.

Diamond and Naomi walked off and went back on the stage to make a little more money. The entire time they were up there, Naomi realized that Trill had his eyes locked on Diamond. Diamond kept on showing out as she did before, not paying him any attention.

When it was over, they walked in the back and did what they needed so they could leave. Before they walked out to go home, Red Man came over to them.

"You did a damn good job out there tonight. They want you back. So, tell me, will we be seeing more of you?"

Diamond looked around where she found the same girls side eyeing her and mugging at her, then looked down at her bag where her money was and said, "Yep. I will definitely be back."

Naomi and Diamond smiled and walked off. Red Man checked Diamond out as he stared constantly at her ass bouncing around in her joggers.

"Now that's a money maker right there. Y'all bitches better tighten up before she take all of y'all clients. Y'all better watch out for her. She ain't playing. She's hungry!" they heard Red Man say to the girls.

On the way home, Diamond and Naomi talked.

"So, what do you think about the club? Did you enjoy yourself tonight?"

"Did I? I fuckin' love it! It wasn't bad at all. It's like I'm getting paid to get drunk and have fun. The part I love most about it is that I make a shit load of money in just a few hours. I don't have to bust my ass on a sorry ass job just to find out that I still don't have enough money two weeks later."

"Yesss, bitch! See, I told you... Girl, the way you showed out tonight, nobody would ever be able to tell that you're an amateur. You did so good out there, and you fit in well!"

"Thanks to you and Joyce. I owe the both of you big time."

"No, I don't want anything in return. I just want you and the twins to be good."

"Thanks, girl!"

"Listen, what was up with ol' boy? He was all over you, girl, and staring hard too. He couldn't take his eyes off you."

"Who, Trill? Girl, please. He was just trying to fuck, and I know it. I can't lie, he is packin' though… ou, girl. I dug in his pants when I gave him a private dance."

The girls high-fived and laughed.

Diamond continued. "If I gave this nigga my pussy, he would be all over me. He already can't take his eyes off of me. I'm not trying to get cuffed so soon. I wanna have some fun."

"I saw how you shut his ass down. I was like, OK, she got this. You handled his ass, and I love it. As long as you keep that same attitude, you will be alright," Naomi said.

Diamond laughed. "He was cute as fuck, but I don't need a nigga right now. Just give me the moneeeey!"

"That's the motive! Just know, there's a lot of niggas like him that comes to the club and try to take advantage. It happens all the time; it even happened to me when I first started. I almost fell victim because I was desperate. I didn't have anyone to put me on game like you do."

"I truly appreciates you!"

"I know you do!" Naomi smiled.

Once they got in the house, they both ran to the couch and emptied their duffel bags. Money scattered and fell everywhere, taking Diamond back to what it was like on stage. It was close to 4 a.m., but those girls didn't give a fuck about that. It didn't bother them much that they were tired and lacked sleep. They were more concerned about how much money they brought home tonight.

Naomi counted her money and left with 2,900. When it was time, Diamond counted the money folded in the rubber band that Trill gave her first which was five hundred alone. Then she counted all the loose bills and it totaled 2,200.

She stared at Naomi. She shook her head then said, "No, no, no, no, no… this can't be right. Wait, let me count this again."

Naomi grabbed Diamond's hand.

"Listen, it's late. I sat here and watched you count it. You didn't fuck up the count! That's the right amount of money, girl."

"On my first night, MiMi?"

"I told you it would happen. When big parties are going on like that, and you dance just as good as you look, it's bound to happen. Don't get used to it though. Some nights will be better than others."

Diamond reached down on the couch, grabbing a handful of money. She shuffled them neatly. She repeatedly grabbed money until she was holding all that she had, hardly fitting her hands around the stack. She alternated frequently with flicking through the stack and pulling it underneath her nose. She closed her eyes and inhaled the scent of perfume, cologne, and weed that lingered on it.

Naomi sat there quietly, yawning constantly, as she watched Diamond having her moment. She knew what it was like, so she kept quiet. She was overjoyed that she could help her friend. Naomi was happy she talked her into going to the club.

"What the hell am I going to do with this money? I've never seen this much money at once before, let alone hold it in my hands. I can't believe this right now. This is a lot of fuckin' money, MiMi!"

"First thing you need to do is get you a new whip and get rid of that raggedy ass one you got. At least get it fixed or something, damn."

Diamond laughed and said, "Yeah, you're right. That car is a piece of shit, ain't it?"

"Now come on, Dream. Let's get ready for bed. We had one hell of a night. I'm tired."

Naomi walked over to Diamond and threw her arm around Diamond's neck.

"I like that name for some reason," she told her.

Chapter 4

"In Love with the Money"

Diamond had only been at the strip club for a month now, but she was already addicted to how fast the money came. She was in deep, but she didn't realize that's what Naomi warned her about in the beginning. Diamond had no plans of leaving the club anytime soon after seeing what she could do for her and her kids with the money she'd already made. She got them a small three-bedroom home just outside of the hood where she grew up. It wasn't in the best shape, but she considered it decent enough for a start.

The more money she got, the more money she spent on things her and the boys never had before. She bought them tons of brand-new shoes and clothes, big screened TVs for every room in the house, she got tablets for the boys and an iPhone for herself. Diamond knew she was splurging and how much she was fucking up the money because often times she regretted having the things she spent the money on. But Diamond didn't care. The smiles on her boys' faces was all that mattered to her.

She went to the club multiple times in the week now, and she already had quite a bit of clientele. It didn't take her long to build it. From the first time she stepped foot on stage, they were mesmerized by her personality, her body, and the way she danced. They showed her just as much love as she showed the poles.

Trill was one of the men that was infatuated with Diamond. Since the very first night he tried hitting on her, he'd been visiting her at the club. After that first dance, he'd been asking to take her out, but she kept brushing him off and giving excuses to why she couldn't. That didn't stop him though. He kept asking and got private dances every night just to get close to her.

Diamond knew the power she had over him, after seeing how badly he wanted her. She knew he would always tip her well for that reason, so she used that to her advantage. She got close to him every time and showed him the attention he desired, all to get the money he was willing to give her.

Naomi constantly pointed out to Diamond how badly Trill wanted her.

"I see how he be looking at you, girl! Before you came, I remember seeing him here, but he has never engaged with the other girls here like how he does you. And another thing, he has never come this often. He really wants you, girl. He sells drugs, but that's about the only bad thing I've heard about him."

Diamond thought about what Naomi told her and wondered if she should consider taking him up on that date he always mentioned. She'd never been on a date and loved the idea of experiencing that, but she didn't want to go out with Trill and get sidetracked on everything she had planned.

"I don't know, MiMi. I don't wanna be fuckin' with no drug dealing ass nigga. I know the kind of reputation they carry and all the hell that comes behind it."

"You keep saying you want money, and that nigga got it. I bet if you fucked with him, he would give it to you without you having to ask; that's how much he is into you, girl. You wouldn't even have to come here and shake your ass anymore, get naked in front of all these bitches and niggas, and you would still get paid! What would you really be losing? Now imagine that."

Naomi continued. "You don't have to be his girlfriend for real. Get what you can out of him and leave. Shit, lead his ass on like he does all these other bitches out here. Give him a dose of his own medicine."

Diamond thought hard about what Naomi was saying. She even thought about what if he never came back after tonight because she wasn't giving in to him. She knew tonight was crucial. He was her highest paying client. There was no way in hell Diamond was willing to take that lost, so she did what she had to do in order to keep him around.

Diamond danced on stage, and they made eye contact multiple times. She was more comfortable at the club now, and her attire showed it. That night, she wore a black lace plunge teddy that covered her highly pigmented areolas, which barely covered her coochie and left her cheeks to hang out completely. She complemented her look with a metallic garter and leg wraps. She stepped in all black five-inch rhinestone covered caged bootie sandal heels that went with her outfit. That was the first time Diamond was so close to being ultimately naked. Trill was loving every bit of it.

Diamond walked over to Trill and led him in the back. As soon as they got in the room for his private session, the deejay played R. Kelly's song "Seems Like You're Ready." Trill was always Diamond's favorite client, but for some reason, that dance felt different.

Diamond danced slowly and grooved to the song that was being played. Trill hyped her up by whispering how good she was at dancing and how delicious she always looked. She already had a thing for him on the low, but all she wanted from him was a good nut and his money.

Trill started getting into the dance and slowly slid his hands underneath her top. He started rubbing on her nipples while she ground on his lap. He gripped her itty-bitty waist tightly as she bounced her ass while he dry humped her. Then when she turned to face him, to grind on him some more, she tilted his neck slightly to the side and kissed on it.

He squeezed on Diamond's ass. He loved how it melted in his hands and how soft and flawless it looked. He was a fool for her, so whatever she allowed him to do, he did, and whatever she was willing to do to him, he enjoyed every moment of it.

When Diamond eased up a little, he stuck his index finger deeply inside of her. As soon as he did, she placed her head back, and she began to moan as her eyes rolled inside of her head. He went in and out of her then quickly found his finger drowning in her tight, warm, wet pussy.

Diamond didn't stop him. He kept going and saw how crazy it made her. He added another finger and went back and forth until he felt her shaking uncontrollably, moaning loudly, and thick, milky cum dripped down his hand.

When it was over, Diamond hopped up. Embarrassment covered her face. She couldn't believe what just happened, but if she could, she would do it all over again.

"I'm... You... I..." Diamond tried speaking, but Trill didn't want her to.

He placed his fingers over her lips and said, "Shhh... don't say a word. It's OK, baby. You didn't do anything wrong. It seemed like you were ready, like R. Kelly said."

Diamond smiled, and her deep dimples turned him on more.

"Listen, I'm tired of running behind you. You work hard as hell in here. Let me just take you out for lunch or dinner. Whatever you want! You pick the place; it's all on me."

Diamond rolled her eyes and started smirking. She wasn't surprised that he asked her again, and she knew what she wanted to do, but she made him think the opposite.

"Since yo' ass won't let up, I guess we can do dinner. I know it might be weird doing a date on a Tuesday night, but I'm off tomorrow. We can do tomorrow night around eight p.m."

"I don't give a fuck what day it is, I'll still take you out! Can I pick you up?"

"Nah, nigga. I'll meet you. Let me hold your phone."

When Trill handed Diamond his phone, she saved her number in it.

"So, tomorrow night at eight p.m., meet me at Hibu Steakhouse."

"Anything you say, beautiful," he told her.

Diamond blushed and shoved Trill's phone to his chest and told him not to be late. Trill loved everything about Diamond, even how hostile and demanding she was at times. He couldn't wait to see what she looked like outside of the club and get the one on one time with her that he'd been dying for.

That night when they were leaving the club, Diamond told Naomi that she had a date with Trill the next night.

"So, you're finally about to give this nigga the time of day." Naomi joked.

Diamond shrugged, "I'm going to enjoy a free night out and see what this nigga is about."

Naomi laughed. "Mmmhmm, I hear ya. That man about to get him some ass tomorrow night."

Diamond lightly pushed Naomi and laughed. "Shut up! I'm not fuckin' him.

The next day, Naomi came over early to help Diamond get ready. Diamond wasn't an expert at any of this. She wanted to look like a bad ass bitch but also didn't want to give him the impression that she was ready to give up some pussy, because she wasn't. She wanted something cute and classy that would take his mind off Dream and get to know her as Diamond.

Naomi took care of Diamond's makeup for her, not that she needed any at all. She had the perfect, warm, chestnut skin complexion that was smooth and free of blemishes. Diamond gave her hair some loose curls, and she decided on a yellow and white short-sleeved crop top, with mid-waist, medium dark, long distressed jeans she cuffed at the bottom, and some cute white sandal styled heels to go with it. She dressed it up with diamond teardrop earrings and a matching bracelet that was far from the real deal. Lastly, she threw on her white faux leather crossbody purse to complement her look.

She went to the mirror and bumped her hair with her hand, running her fingers through her curls and popping her lush lips constantly to make sure her nude lipstick was applied evenly. She turned around to see how her booty looked then turned back around to make sure the look she had was what she was going for.

"Damn! OK already! You look great! Now get out of here before you're late!" Naomi hollered.

"Come on, boys. Kiss your mommy goodbye." Naomi continued.

The boys ran to Diamond, hugging each of her legs. They told her how pretty she looked and how much they loved her. After Diamond hugged and kissed them, Naomi pushed her out the door.

"I'll call to check on you. If you don't answer at least three of my calls, I'm packing the boys up and coming to find you," Naomi said.

Diamond laughed. "I got you," she replied then got in her car.

Diamond sat in the car and turned her key. She found contentment in starting her car, now that she didn't have to worry about it not working like it should. She screamed in the car and wiggled in her seat. She was happy as hell. *Tonight is gonna be a good night,* she told herself.

When she pulled up in the parking lot, she texted him, after realizing she didn't know what kind of car he drove and vice versa. Once she sent the text, he called. As soon as she answered, she heard a knock on her window.

When she looked over, it was Trill. She hung up her phone and rolled down the window.

"Why the hell would you do that? Damn! You scared me."

"I'm sorry, baby. I didn't mean to scare you."

He opened her car door and rolled her window back up.

"Come on, beautiful. Let's go inside," he told her.

Diamond stepped out of the car, and he eyed her from her head down to her toes. When she got out the car completely, she swung her hair and fixed her pants, pulling them up in the back. Trill couldn't help but to look. Hell, it was hard for anyone to miss all the ass Diamond carried.

Trill's eyes were stuck to Diamond. He ran his tongue over his lips and said, "Damn, girl. You look good." Diamond smiled, showing off her pretty white teeth and dimples that were sucked deeply into her cheeks. He was in such a daze, he forgot he still held her car door opened.

"Thanks, boo. Now close my door so I can lock it."

"My bad," he told her.

Diamond walked ahead of him, until he ran to catch up with her.

He walked beside her and complimented her on the way. It left Diamond flattered, so she thanked him and blushed.

No matter how much she played hard to get, she couldn't ignore how sexy he looked in his Fendi outfit and Balenciaga shoes to match. Every time Trill moved, she was blinded by his diamond stud earrings and gold rope necklace that shined brightly from the streetlights. He was looking fine as hell, and she was feeling quite lucky to have him by her side. She'd never dealt with anyone like him before.

Trill opened the door of the restaurant for her. Shortly after arriving, they were seated. They both took a menu and glanced over it, trying to decide what would satisfy their appetites best. Diamond knew she wasn't spending, so she got exactly what she wanted. She ordered a T-bone steak with grilled shrimp, a lobster tail on the side, and some broccoli and cheese. She even got a light frozen alcoholic beverage while she waited.

Trill had money, so he didn't give a damn about how much of it she spent. He was trying to win her over anyways. He didn't order near as much as Diamond did. Instead, he kept it simple with BBQ ribs with bacon and cheese mashed potatoes.

"So, baby girl, I know you go by Dream, but do I have to call you that outside of the club?"

"Nah, I'm Diamond."

"Damn, that name fits you perfectly. How old are you?"

"I'm twenty-one. I just had a birthday."

"I would have never thought. You carry yourself like a grown ass woman, and you have a body like one too."

Diamond blushed.

"So what is your young ass doing dancing in the club?"

"I gotta make money! Young? Well, nigga, how old are you?"

Trill started grinning. "Old enough to be yo' daddy," he joked. "Nah, I'm thirty."

"Well damn!"

"That's too old?"

"No, you're good. Ain't like I've never dealt with an older guy before."

"What's the oldest guy you've dealt with?"

"My baby daddy was eight years older than me."

"Baby daddy? How many kids do you have?"

"Two boys. They're twins. Jordan and Joshua. They are five years old."

"That's what's up. So do you have any siblings?" Trill continued.

Diamond put her head down. It was still a sensitive topic for her to talk about, making it hard for her to discuss at times.

"Yes... I have one brother who I lost to gun violence a few years ago."

"Damn! Are you good?"

"Yeah, I am. It's still hard for me."

It got silent, and Diamond took a napkin to stop her tears from ruining her makeup.

"I'm sorry."

"No need to apologize, beautiful. I should be the one apologizing to you."

Diamond's eyes grew wide, not understanding what Trill was talking about.

"For what?"

"For asking."

"Well you can't apologize for something you knew nothing about. I'm sure not many women sit before you and say that. I guess it's just my luck."

Diamond switched the subject, trying to get the spotlight off her.

"Enough about me. What about you? Do you have kids? Where do you live? What do you do for a living, 'cause you always got money?"

"Well… I have two daughters. My youngest is Nevaeh. She's three years old. My oldest is Nyasia, and she's thirteen. They are my heart."

The waitress brought their food out to them. Diamond wasn't shy to dive in and stuff her face, so she did as she continued to get to know him.

"So do they have the same mom?"

"No, they don't."

"What about my other question? Are you gonna ignore it?"

Trill started smiling, showing off his gold teeth. He continued chewing and began shuffling around in his seat. He looked up at Diamond and said, "I'm a businessman."

Naomi had already tipped Diamond off at the beginning about him being a big-time drug dealer, but Diamond played along. She was far from the fool he thought she was.

"So, what kind of business do you have?"

"Retail."

"Mmm… OK," Diamond said, leaving it at that.

"You know you're too fuckin' beautiful to be showing your body off for money in front of them bustas, right? When do you plan on giving that up?"

"Well, it pays the bills, so no time soon. I've struggled long enough. My life has finally taken a turn for the better."

"Hmm… I see."

"It seems like you're bothered by what I do. Why? You go there all the time for that reason, don't you?"

"I'm not bothered. I'm good. With a nigga like me in your life, you'll understand where I'm coming from real soon."

"What's that supposed to mean?"

"You'll see. Are you ready to go? I gotta good club we can go to after we leave here."

"Yeah, I'm full. The food is good every time. I love coming here."

"You know what's crazy? This is one of my favorite spots too," Trill told her.

"Wow, we have something in common," she replied.

Once Trill paid, they left out and headed to the parking lot. Diamond walked toward her car with the intentions of following Trill to the place where they were going.

"Where are you going, girl?"

"To my car. What do you mean?"

"I'll drive you."

"I don't know about all of that."

"Do you think I'm going to kidnap or hurt you? I'm not that type of nigga."

"Shit, I don't really know you like that, so ain't no tellin'. I don't even know where you are taking me."

"Girl, quit playin'. C'mon, I'll drive. You're good. Just know whenever you're with me, you are safe, no matter where we go. I'm respected in these streets."

Diamond decided to ride with Trill. He took her to his darkly tinted all-black Challenger, with the chrome rims and beige interior.

"Damn, is this you?" Diamond asked Trill as she circled around the car, checking the license plate on the low to send to Naomi.

"You like it?"

"I love it! This shit is nice."

Trill opened the passenger door for her, and she dropped in the seat. Diamond immediately got on her phone and texted Naomi, letting her know what was going on and the license plate number to his car before she forgot. Trill looked over to Diamond and asked her if everything was OK.

"Yeah. I'm just checking on my kids," she lied.

"OK. If you need to leave early, let me know."

"I will. Listen, where are you taking me?"

"Have you ever heard of any of the clubs in the uptown?"

"Yeah, I've heard of a few."

"There's one called Royalty."

"It ain't a hole in the wall is it? 'Cause I ain't trying to get shot tonight."

"No, girl. I wouldn't put you in harm's way. Everything will be fine, I promise."

Diamond and Trill went into the club. It was a decent size, with a nice crowd. It was chill, for the most part, and Trill got them a VIP section so they wouldn't be standing all night.

"Stay here. I'll be right back," he told her.

While Trill went to the bar, Diamond texted Naomi the name of the club and what color car he drove. She didn't have a bad vibe from him, but she was still nervous, being that men were crazy as hell these days, and as of yet, there was no telling what type of man he was.

Naomi stayed up and texted Diamond to make sure she was OK. In fact, she told Diamond that she would be up all night, until she got home. Naomi didn't trust Trill any more than Diamond did. When Diamond saw Trill coming back, she sent a quick text to Naomi, letting her know she had to go and that she'd be home soon.

"This is a really good drink. I know you like fruity drinks from what you ordered a little while ago, so try this."

Diamond grabbed the cup from him and put it to her nose. It smelled good to her, but she was nervous to drink being that she didn't watch him with it at the bar. She was still uneasy about him selling drugs and wondered if any ended up in her drink. She held the drink in her hand still.

"It's Rum Punch. They have the best here, I'm telling you. It's fruity like you like it, but it gives you a nice buzz."

Diamond sipped the drink a little and realized she didn't feel funny afterwards. It was her first time drinking it, but she liked it and downed the rest quickly.

"Get me another," she told him.

Trill looked at Diamond. He knew what it would do to her, but she didn't, so he tried warning her.

"You might want to wait," he told her, but she insisted that he got more, so he did. Shortly after he came back with her drink, she was finished with that one too.

Diamond started feeling the music and started dancing in her seat. Trill threw back his shots of gin then got closer to her.

"Do you wanna get up and dance?" he asked.

Diamond rose from her seat, threw her arm in the air, and started dancing. She twerked in front of Trill, while he sat back and watched her. Then she started grinding on him, similar to what she did to him in the strip club. The only difference was, he wasn't obligated to pay her this time. He was enjoying what she was doing while he also observed how she acted on liquor. Like any man, he thought about what he could possibly do to her since she was drunk. Maybe get some head from her or take her back to his place and get inside of her. But he didn't want to fuck it up with her so soon. *Should I do what I want or keep it chill?* he asked himself.

Diamond led him to the dance floor where she rocked up on him some more. She was shaking her ass on him, while he stood firmly, handling her. She danced nonstop for about an hour before she asked Trill for another drink.

They went to the bar to get one more. Trill took her back to the VIP section so she could calm down. She sat on his lap, facing him, resting her head on his shoulders. She rubbed her fingers slowly across his clean-cut mocha skin. She began sucking on his neck passionately.

He knew what that did to him every time, and Diamond found out too, after feeling him getting bigger in the pants right underneath her pussy. Trill pulled Diamond's head up slowly and told her that he was taking her home. Diamond agreed and stood up to leave. When she got up, she stumbled, so Trill wrapped his arm around hers to keep her from hitting the floor.

He put Diamond in the passenger seat of the car. After pulling off, he asked her where she lived, but she wasn't drunk enough to tell.

"Just take me to my car," she told him.

He didn't think that was a good idea, but he didn't argue with her either; he did as he was told. While he drove, he turned the music on to break the silence. When he pulled up to the parking lot next to Diamond's car, he asked her, "So, how did you enjoy our night?"

"It was fun."

"Good. I'm glad you enjoyed yourself. You liked the Rum Punch too, I see."

Diamond started laughing. "So, you got jokes, huh? It was good. It snuck up on me though. I wasn't expecting that. At first, I wasn't feeling much of anything, but after drinking more than one, the buzz hit me at once," she continued.

"I was trying to tell you that, but you didn't want to listen," Trill said as he parked the car.

"Yeah, I'm hardheaded sometimes," Diamond admitted.

Trill grinned. He started staring into Diamond's russet brown eyes, and Diamond stared back into his without saying a word. Trill grabbed Diamond's chin and leaned in to kiss her, and without thinking, she kissed him back. He used his other hand to push his seat all the way back, then slightly gripped her shirt to pull her closer toward him.

Diamond lifted up, and she managed to get on top of him in the driver's seat. As they continued to kiss, Trill took Diamond's shirt off. He rubbed on her titties while she unbuckled his belt and unzipped his pants. She started caressing his balls with her hand and felt that he was already hard. Trill unstrapped Diamond's bra and told her to get up for just a second.

While he slid on a rubber, she took one leg out of her jeans. He sucked Diamond's titties as she moaned intensely and rubbed her pussy on his dick, feeling what she could through her panties. He kept sucking on her titties and started rubbing her pussy. Diamond was enjoying the pleasurable moment they were having.

After he felt how wet she was, he slid her panties to the side. With just getting the head in alone, his eyes started rolling backwards. He was shocked to feel how tight her pussy was, for such a stripper. He wasn't expecting that from the experience he had with strippers he'd dealt with in the past.

Trill thrust his body against hers, forcing himself inside of her just a little bit more with every stroke. He was ready to pound her pussy. He knew he had to have it just from feeling the little bit he'd already felt. Diamond moaned and bounced continually, and with the scent of Trill's cologne lingering around the car, it turned her on more. As soon as he got it all in, he only got four deep strokes before Diamond eased up off him. She was guilty about what they were doing after knowing him for just a month.

"I can't! I can't!" She tried explaining. Trill placed his hands around her waist, pushing her down more as he refused to stop so soon.

"You can't what? Take this dick?"

Diamond didn't answer; instead, she continued to moan. She was still bouncing on top of him. Truth was, she was loving how good sex was with him. The last person she'd fucked was her kids' father, many years ago. She forgot how good sex could be and what dick inside of her vagina felt like.

She and Trill had been going for some time, and she never tried stopping him again. With all the drinks she had and how good Trill made her feel, it brought the freak out of her. Diamond started bouncing faster and tightened her vaginal muscles, making Trill moan louder than she did.

"Uh... yeah, baby, that's it... uh. Keep going, baby. Keep going!" Trill hollered.

Trill wasn't expecting Diamond to fuck him like that. She gave him a wild ride he was sure to remember. Within five minutes of them sexing, Trill nutted. He was mad at himself for it happening so soon, but it was nothing he could do, being inside a hole so good.

Diamond kept going until she got hers, leaving Trill shocked. He didn't know who the hell Diamond was anymore. He didn't have much strength left, but Diamond didn't let up a bit. When she was getting ready to bust her nut, she began to holler loudly. She moaned constantly and grasped tightly onto everything she got her hands on. She threw her head back, running her nails across his ceiling and started shaking continuously.

"Oh shit... Oh shit! Yeeesssssss... Uhhhh... Ouuuu!" she hollered.

Once she was done, she got up off him, slid her shirt back on, and placed her panties back in the place they never should have moved from in the first place. After she put her leg back into her pants, she leaned over in the passenger seat to grab her phone and her purse, then hopped out of the car. Trill tried fixing himself quickly enough to follow behind her.

"Damn, baby, you a beast," Diamond heard Trill saying behind her. She stopped and turned around to face him.

"Don't ever underestimate me because of my age. It ain't nothin' but a number."

Trill stood beside his car with his hands folded behind his head. He watched Diamond walk back to her car, not wasting any time to lock his eyes on her ass once more. As he focused on her, he stood in the parking lot with his pants that had fallen damn near to his ankles. He bit on his lips, thinking about their next time.

He watched Diamond get in her car and stood in the same spot after she had already drove off. "That bitch is a beast." He whispered to himself as he walked back to the driver's side of his car.

Chapter 5

"Control Your Hoes"

When Diamond got in the house, the boys were asleep, but Naomi was still awake, lying on the couch, watching TV.

"Damn, you must have had yourself a good time. You didn't look like this when you left." Naomi joked.

Diamond tossed her keys on the coffee table in the center of her living room and exhaled as she dropped on the couch next to Naomi.

"So, how was it?" Naomi asked.

Diamond sat on the chair silently for a moment, then looked at Naomi out the corner of her eyes.

Naomi sat up in the chair, eager to know how Diamond's night went. She kept asking questions until Diamond decided to answer her.

"What happened?" Naomi asked.

Diamond placed her forehead in the palm of her hand. She already knew what Naomi's response would be once she found out Diamond was a really bad girl tonight. Still, Diamond didn't say a word. Diamond was acting strange, so Naomi already had an idea of what happened.

"Nooo! Don't tell me you did what I think you did!"

Diamond still didn't say anything. She got up from the couch and stumbled to the bathroom to pee. Unknowingly, Naomi followed right behind. Naomi stood in the doorway of the bathroom, still trying to get answers out of Diamond. Diamond looked up from the toilet seat and rolled her eyes.

"Alright, alright. Yeah, I did what you're thinking. Damn! But it was by accident. Man, I was drunk, OK. By the time it happened, it was too late to stop, so I kept going!"

Naomi stood with both hands over her mouth.

"After all these years, you finally got yourself some. I told you he was gonna' knock the cobwebs off your pussy!"

Diamond stared at Naomi while still sitting on the toilet and burst out laughing.

"So tell me. Was he worth it? Was it good?"

"Hell yeah… and my nut was too!"

Naomi started jumping and screaming loudly in excitement. She quickly quieted herself down after realizing the boys were in the house asleep.

"I can't believe you fucked him. And it was in the car! Oh, so you're nasty nasty?" Naomi joked.

"I had to get it where I could. I damn sure wasn't bringing that nigga here and have him knowing where I live."

"All I'm gonna say is, don't get trapped, sis."

"I won't! This is the last time, for real, but how he was acting, I know he's gonna' want more. I'm not going to do it again though."

Naomi gave her the side eye.

"For real, I'm not," Diamond argued.

"Yeah, yeah. You already gave it up, and from how you're talkin', it sounds like he got some make a bitch crazy, can't leave him alone dick."

"Mmm… yeah… maybe… something like that, but I'm not about to be one of those bitches that's all over him and dick."

***

When Diamond went to work on Friday, her and Naomi rode together. Diamond continued with her routine as she normally did. While she was in the locker room, getting dressed, she thought about him.

After they fucked, it was hard for her to get him off her mind. I mean really, how would that be easy for any woman? To have a fine nigga with good dick and a lot of money was damn near every bitch's dream to have.

When it was time to go on stage, she stuck closely to Naomi. She couldn't seem to get in the groove of things at first, but once she went to get a few drinks, she began to focus. It was like a normal night for her. She saw Trill, but she ignored him. Every time she would glance at him, he had his eyes on her. He sat back in the VIP section he always sat in and eyed her like a hawk. Wherever she went, his eyes followed. He didn't let her out of his sight.

When it was time for their break, Diamond walked off stage with her head down. She was so focused on not dropping the money she grabbed from her bra and garter, that she wasn't paying attention to her surroundings. As soon as she looked up, Trill was standing in front of her. She jumped and stopped in her tracks. He never came on that side of the club, so to see him there, she knew something was up.

"Damn, nigga, you scared me," she told him.

"Can I get my dance now?" he asked firmly.

"What is up with you? You've been acting strange all night. You really need to chill," she replied.

Trill rubbed his nose, fixed his shirt, and threw back whatever it was he had in his cup.

"Nah, I'm good. Do you have time for me now?"

"I have time for all my paying clients. What you mean? I got you after our break."

Diamond walked off from him and continued on about her way. When she walked up beside Naomi at her locker, she gave her the scoop about Trill.

"I'm about ready to go home. I'm not feeling this shit tonight," Diamond told her.

"What's wrong?"

Diamond whispered. "Girl, ol' boy trippin'. He is acting funny. He's been watching me all night, he popped up on me, and he's talkin' to me crazy. What the fuck is up with him?"

"You already know what it is. You done gave him some young born-again virgin pussy, now his ass buggin'. Since he know what you are workin' wit' now, he probably don't want these other niggas getting close to you."

Diamond nudged Naomi in her side and started laughing. "He needs to chill. He's really making me regret doing that shit."

"Really?" Naomi asked sarcastically.

"Hell no," Diamond replied. They both laughed about it while they left out of the locker room. On their way back out, Diamond saw Trill still standing where she left him. Diamond parted ways with Naomi and went in the back to give him his dance.

As soon as they got in the room, Diamond pushed Trill down in the seat. She threw her legs over his lap to sit on him, then he whispered in her ear. "Do me like you did me the other night."

Diamond was drunk, but she couldn't ignore that he was wearing her favorite scent. With the position she was in, she started reminiscing on how good he made her feel that night. He gripped her tightly by the waist. She closed her eyes, held the back of his neck with both of her hands, and worked her hips.

Trill knew she'd been drinking, and he knew how she got now with the right amount. Trill got hard almost instantly, and with no one in the room with them this time, he tried her by pulling his dick completely out of his pants, wagging it from side to side.

"Come on, baby, you know you want it."

Diamond looked at it for a while and got wetter. She knew she wanted to hop on it, but she was trying to be firm on making the last time their last time like she promised Naomi.

"Hell no, nigga. I'm at work. What the fuck is you thinkin'?"

"Well what about tonight when you get off?"

"I don't know. I'll think about it. What about my money though? Ain't shit free!" Diamond reminded him.

Trill handed Diamond three hundred dollars.

"Is this all you got?"

Trill nodded his head, and Diamond walked off from him highly disappointed. She knew he had more. She was almost 100 percent sure he was slacking because he was in his feelings tonight. She didn't trip though; she was one of the most loved dancers in the building. Although Trill decided to play with her money, she still took home a hefty amount.

Diamond was done for the night and went in the back along with all the other girls to gather her things to leave. When Diamond first walked in, she could feel the tension, and she knew something wasn't right. The same girls who seemed to not like her since day one was side eyeing her again.

They still didn't like Diamond from the very first time she stepped foot in the club as a dancer. In fact, after they saw how the men flocked to her and how much money she made as a newbie, they resented her more. Diamond wasn't a confrontational chick though, so she let it slide.

One of the girls walked past Diamond and bumped her arm, making Diamond drop one of her heels that she was putting in the locker. Diamond looked at Naomi, and she noticed how angry Naomi got. She knew that wouldn't be the end of that.

"What the fuck is your problem?" Naomi asked Treasure.

Treasure looked back at Naomi and Diamond, smirking while walking back to her area.

"Just let it go, MiMi. It ain't that serious," Diamond told her.

"Hell no! We ain't no fuckin' punks. I'm gonna check this bitch if you don't!"

Diamond decided to go over to Treasure instead of letting Naomi.

"Listen, I know what you did was intentional, and I know you don't like me for whatever reason. I could care less if you do or if you don't, but all I'm gonna say is, keep yo' fuckin' hands off of me. This is your final warning."

After Diamond said what she said, Naomi followed her back to their locker.

"This bitch fucked one of her clients and grew some balls," Treasure joked. "Yeah, bitch! I saw you out with ol' boy that night, at Royalty. So tell me, how much did he pay you?" Treasure continued.

Diamond's eyes widened, and she looked at Naomi. Nobody was supposed to know that she was fucking with Trill on the low. It surprised her how quickly it got out. Diamond was stunned by what Treasure said. Diamond knew she wanted trouble because Treasure kept running her mouth.

"You ain't special, bitch! Everybody in this motherfucker probably already fucked with Trill. Shit, I know I did. He was all up in this pussy. You ain't nothing but another piece of pussy to him. Don't let the shit he put in your ear boost you up to think you the best thing walking around here. You ain't no better than the rest of us," Treasure said.

Diamond wasn't having it. She got in a rage and charged at Treasure.

Diamond rolled up on Treasure and pointed two fingers in her face. "Listen, bitch, watch your fuckin' mouth."

"Ouu! I'm scared," Treasure said sarcastically.

Diamond started laughing as she turned around and looked at the group of women.

"See, her problem is she's a jealous ass bitch. Yeah, he pays me well and offered to take me out, but she's mad all he did was fuck her droopy pussy and left her. Sounds like she's highly upset that I'm getting the attention he never showed her."

The girls started laughing, and as soon as Diamond was about to continue on, Treasure hit her in the back of the head with a beer bottle. Out of nowhere, Naomi hopped in and started beating on Treasure. Treasure's girls jumped in, and although Diamond wasn't friends with any of the other girls, they helped her and Naomi since they were cool and outnumbered.

A few girls ran out to get Red Man and the security so they could break up the fight. It was a huge brawl in the locker room over jealousy and purposeless hate. Treasure wanted to be the top bitch in the club. She'd been there the longest and was mad at how new girls came in, took over some of her clients, and made more money than she did.

She did the same to Naomi when she first came. Even most of the other girls too. She'd ran many girls out of the club. They left because of Treasure's attitude and bullying. Naomi, on the other hand, was one of the few that wasn't standing for that and wasn't going to let it happen to her best friend either.

Treasure was a pure bitch! She always had an attitude. Even when she was on the floor, it didn't change anything. She was at fault for why she wasn't making as much money as the rest of the girls. The girls would always overhear guys complaining about her. Hell, they didn't want shit to do with her either. She was well experienced and had a nice body, but customers couldn't put up with her attitude.

When Red Man and the security guards came back in, they separated the girls.

"This is some bullshit! Gather y'all shit so y'all can get the fuck out!" Red Man yelled. "What was this about anyways?"

Nobody spoke. Instead, everybody gathered what they needed and started heading out the door. Diamond and Naomi started heading out too, but Red Man grabbed their arms.

"Not so fast! Tell me what's going on. I don't allow this shit in my club, and Naomi, you already know this."

"Red Man, I'm going to be straight up with you. I've been working with you for a long time now, and we both know who the problem came from and who is to blame. My girl here ain't even wit' all that drama shit, but that big bully bitch over there, ha! This ain't the first time she's fought in this damn club, and you know that. Better check your girl. If not, I will tell you right now. If she thinks she's gonna bully or lay hands on my girl, I will knock her ass clean out every single time she tries. She ain't gon' play wit' a damn soul over here."

Red Man looked at Treasure the entire time Naomi was speaking because he knew she was a problem. Nobody understood why he kept her around though. Truth was, she was fucking him to keep her job. They were messing around on the low, but he didn't take her serious. Shit, no man did, which was why she was still lonely and single at thirty-six years old.

"I'll take care of her," Red Man told Naomi. "Diamond, take a day or two off and gather yourself. I know this was a hell of an experience. Call me if you need me."

"No! Hold up! You can't stop my girl money because of—"

Diamond interrupted Naomi. "Girl, it's cool. I'll take the two days."

Naomi looked at Diamond like she was crazy, but she couldn't argue with her decision. She was a grown ass woman, and it was her time and money she was jeopardizing after all. Naomi looked back at Treasure once more right before snatching her bag off the counter. Diamond locked her locker and followed Naomi out.

They headed out the back door and walked to the car.

"I can't believe you are about to take those days off. Don't let her scare you."

"MiMi, I'm not scared. I do need the time to cool off and chill. I can't remember the last time I fought. I barely fought as a kid, but here I am fighting as a grown ass woman over some shit she's jealous of me for. If I come back tomorrow, I might want to pop her in the face again. This bitch done fucked up my wig I took my time with. Can you believe this shit?" Diamond continued.

"Yeah, I warned you about those bitches."

"You sure did, but I didn't know Treasure was like that. What do you think it's really about though? It can't be the money."

"It's no telling with her. What I really think it is though, is Trill. Sounds like they parted ways on bad terms, or they are still messing around. You need to check him about this. You can't be getting yourself into shit when that's not even your nigga."

"Aye, beautiful." They heard a man's voice from across the parking lot.

"Speaking of the devil himself," Naomi said.

It was Trill. He was trying to get Diamond's attention. He didn't forget about her and what she said about giving up pussy once she got off. He waited around for her for almost an hour to see what she decided. Little did he know, one of his bitches had already ruined that for him.

"Devil? No, girl. I'm the nigga all the females dream of having, probably even you."

"That's a fuckin' lie," Naomi said quickly.

"Ain't that right, baby girl?" he asked Diamond.

Diamond rolled her eyes as Naomi stood beside them laughing before she walked off.

"I'll be waiting in the car. Remember what I told you! Take care of it!" Naomi hollered.

Trill looked at Diamond and saw she was bleeding.

"What the hell happened to you? What is she talking about? Are you all right?" he asked her.

Diamond felt something on her lip, so she patted it with her hand and looked at it. It was blood dripping.

"Yeah, I'm OK. I got into a fight with one of the girls named Treasure. She brought your name up right before we fought. Do you deal with her?"

"What did she say?"

"Answer my question!"

"I don't, but I have. She's my youngest daughter mother. She's still in love with me, but we are over."

"Emm… ok. I'm not about to do this shit. We aren't together, and look at all the drama I'm already in, all because she saw us together the other night. I'm not about to do this."

Diamond started walking off to the car where Naomi waited for her, but Trill grabbed her by her bag, stopping her.

"Do what?"

"This, Trill! I'm not fighting your baby mama because she's jealous of something we don't even have together. I have to work here! This is how I take care of my kids and pay my bills! I'm not about to come to work and deal with this drama every night. This ain't why I came here."

"Listen, I'll take care of her. Let me make it up to you. Tell your friend I'll bring you home. Just let me explain."

Diamond stood in the parking lot with her arms crossed as she thought about if she wanted to go with him or not. She wasn't in the mood much for his company, but she wanted to hear him out, and she was hungry.

"Come on, baby. Are you gonna at least let me explain?"

Diamond walked over to Naomi. Naomi rolled the window down, and Diamond leaned in.

"Treasure is his baby mama," Diamond told her.

"Damn, for real? Well, no wonder why she's in her feelings."

"Yeah. And he wants to make it up to me and explain their situation. He says he'll drop me off home. What do you think I should do?"

"Whatever you want. If you go, just please keep in touch, and let me know that you are safe. And don't stay out all night."

"Alright. I guess I'll go. Unlock the door."

Diamond threw her bag in the back seat and told her she would see her in an hour and a half.

"What about your head?" Naomi asked.

"I'll take care of it," Diamond told her.

"Please be safe, girl."

"I will!" Diamond hollered.

Diamond walked over to Trill and told him all she had to spare was an hour and a half. When she got in the car, he started explaining to her, as he promised.

"Treasure is a trip. I met her at a club, not this one. She was working at another club at the time. We knew each other for about six months, but we only dated for two. A little after the two months, she got pregnant with my daughter. We were just fuckin' around and chillin'; we had no plans on any of that shit happening. After she had the baby, she wanted a relationship, and we tried it out, but it only lasted four months. She started working here, and that's when I found out she fucked Red Man for her job. She refused to leave the club, so I refused to stick around. Our daughter is three, and she hardly comes on to me, but when she sees that I'm interested in other woman, she tries to fuck that up for me."

"So, when were you going to tell me this?"

"I didn't think it mattered. We aren't together. But now that I know she's wilding on you like this, I figured you should know. I like you a lot. I've never dealt with any strippers besides her. It's usually a hit it and quit it thing with them. I don't take them on dates, explain shit to them, or even mention my kids. This shit with you is way more than that."

"Why me?"

"You are different. A man can tell who a woman really is just by looking at her. From the first time I saw you, I knew you were different. By how you look, talk, and dance. It's nothing wrong with any of that, but I know that you aren't anything like those other girls. I've never seen you around in the clubs or streets, and none of my boys know you. That's a good thing. Your name ain't all over the streets, and I like that."

"You're right. I just started dancing here, actually. My friend convinced me to come work here. At first, I was hesitant about it, but it turned out not to be so bad. Besides, I needed the money. I make way more here than I did at Burger King."

"You think what you make at the club is money? Fuck wit' me so I can show you what real money is."

"I'm not a goal digger or a prostitute."

Trill started laughing. "I didn't label you as either. I'm just trying to look out since that seems to be the biggest problem you have. You are better than this club shit. You don't need to be there. I like you so much. Do you think you would want a relationship with me?"

"I don't know. I'm not looking for a relationship right now. We can be friends. I don't want to rush into anything, and with the tension between me and your daughter's mom, I don't think it's a good idea."

"I'll handle her; you don't worry. We can take it slow. I'm not trippin' about that."

They pulled up to Waffle House since it wasn't much of anything still open that time of night. Trill got out and waited for Diamond to follow.

"Do you expect me to go in there looking like this?"

"Oh shit, I forgot. It's not that bad though. Just go in the bathroom, clean it up, and put your wig on."

Diamond took Trill's advice and met him at the table. She sat silently, thinking about all that happened. With the information she had, she tried putting the pieces of the puzzle together, but she still didn't feel like everything was adding up.

"What's wrong, beautiful?" he asked.

"I'm just tired. It's been a long night. Can we get to-go instead?"

"Sure. The food shouldn't take much longer, and I'll get you home shortly."

Diamond gave him a half smile and told him thank you. When they got their food and left, Trill dropped her off at her place. She gave him a tight hug and got out of the car.

"Can I come inside?"

"No, not tonight; maybe some other time. Thanks for everything, though. Good night," she told him and went inside.

Chapter 6

"Money make her world turn"

It wasn't much that Diamond could do when it came to keeping her relationship with Trill on a friendly level after he showered her with gifts. He would send her gifts to the club and still sit in the crowd and watch her dance as if nothing ever happened. He still got his lap dances from her like he normally did and still tipped her well. Often times when she was home, she got random gifts to her door front, such as edible arrangements and bouquets of flowers.

Diamond didn't let the situation with Treasure bother her or come between her and Trill's friendship. Trill knew all along that he wanted Diamond on his side, but he knew it wouldn't be easy to get her. Giving up was not an option. Diamond wasn't realizing that everything Trill was doing for her would benefit him in the end. She was so caught up in everything he could give her and the way he laid the pipe that she forgot about the plan she had in the beginning.

Diamond sat on her porch to catch fresh air while her boys were in school, and an Uber pulled up in front of her door. Diamond began to get nervous with no idea of who it could be. She quickly got up and went inside to watch from her living room window. Moments later, she saw Trill get out of the car. *What the hell is he doing in an Uber? Better yet, what the hell is he doing here period?* she asked herself.

Since their date, she and Trill had been spending more time together over the past two months. During that time, she'd been welcoming him over, but this was the first time he showed up unannounced. She got up and ran to the door, getting to it before he was able to knock.

"What the hell are you doing here?"

"I wanted to surprise you."

She looked down at his hands, only to find it empty. She looked around on the porch, but nothing was there either. She looked along the streets, but there was only his Uber still sitting in front of her driveway.

"With what?" she asked.

"Put on your shoes, and I'll show you."

Diamond threw on some slippers she had next to the door, locked the door behind her, and followed Trill to the Uber. During the ride, Diamond started asking what she wanted to know.

"Where is your car?"

"I won't be needing it today," he told her, smiling.

"What's going on? Where are you taking me?"

"Have I ever done anything wrong to you?"

"No."

"OK then. This time is no different. Sit back and enjoy the ride. Soon your suspicious thoughts will have your face glowing with a smile that will wrap around your entire beautiful face. Just trust me on this."

He played it so enticingly, Diamond was yearning to know where she was going. She sat back as she was told, but her mind was still racing. So many thoughts ran through her head, since she had no clue what to expect. Just moments later, the Uber pulled up to the Mercedes Benz car lot. Diamond looked over to Trill, where he sat next to her smiling. Diamond patted on Trill's leg continuously in excitement.

"Quit playing! Quit playing with me! This must be a damn joke!" she said excitedly.

When she felt the Uber driver slowing down, Diamond had already opened the car door before the car was at a complete stop. She stood on the lot, looking around. So much excitement filled her eyes. She resembled a kid in a candy store.

"Pick whichever you want," Trill told her.

Diamond didn't waste any time running up to one of the cars she had her eyes on. That was until she noticed the number of digits on the car window. She looked over to Trill and pointed at it.

"You said whatever I wanted, but this car says sixty-nine thousand dollars. Are you sure? I can't be held responsible for these payments if you don't pay the—"

"Listen, baby, you ain't gotta worry. I said whatever you want. Bosses don't give a fuck about a price and damn sure don't make payments. If you want something, then get it. I need you to know, once we leave this lot with whatever car you choose, we don't owe these motherfuckers shit!"

Diamond started to get moist in the panties. What Trill said and the tone of voice he spoke to her in, turned her on. She'd dreamt about driving a Mercedes for almost all her life. She never thought she'd be standing on a lot full of luxury cars at twenty-one years old. She was used to driving preowned cars that cost no more than $1,500 that were classified as lemons. She didn't think she was good enough to have a car so valuable.

She decided on a silver Mercedes E350 after seeing the features it had and realizing how good she looked in it. The 1997 Camry she drove was in no comparison to this.

"So, what do you think?" she asked.

"Is this it? Is this the car you want?" Trill asked her.

"Yes! This is it!"

Trill looked at the salesman and said, "We'll take it."

Nodding, the salesman said, "Great! Let's head inside to make the sale final." They both got out of the car and followed behind him.

"So, whose name is the car going in?" the salesman asked them.

Trill looked at Diamond and saw her shrugging her shoulders.

"It will be in my name, sir," Trill said.

"OK. Great. The total after taxes, tags, and dealer fee are $76,458. How much are we putting down today? The minimum for that vehicle is roughly around eight thousand dollars. Will that be an issue?"

"Uh, just wait a minute, sir," Diamond told the salesman.

"That's a lot of money for just one car. I don't have to have a brand-new car or a Mercedes. Let's go someplace cheaper," Diamond whispered to Trill.

"Sit back and be quiet. I got this."

Trill slid the duffel bag off his shoulders, and he immediately noticed the salesman getting nervous. With Trill's persona and him having a duffel bag, the poor guy thought he was about to be robbed or gunned down. Diamond looked at him apprehensively as well. She didn't know what was in the bag and what Trill was about to do next. Trill dropped the bag on the desk and unzipped it slowly. The salesman slowly backed up, and Diamond slid to the edge of her seat.

"I doubt there will be any issues, don't you?" Trill told the salesman. The guy got up slowly and looked inside of the bag. He stared at Trill as if he'd never seen anything like it before. Diamond stood up and glanced in the bag as well, curious to know what it was the salesman was infatuated with.

There were stacks and stacks of blue Benjamins wrapped in rubber bands. Trill dropped in the chair as he watched the two of them standing over the money. "Let's close this deal," he told them.

After Trill bought Diamond the car, he saw how happy she was with him and made her feel like she was obligated to stay with him after he spent so much money on her. She knew she couldn't fuck up with him now that she had no job and had gotten rid of the car she owned in her name.

Diamond quit the club to be with Trill more and make him happy. She kept the boys with Ms. Mable, so whenever she wanted to go with Trill, she could. Trill plan had worked. When he realized that he'd won her over, they made things official.

***

Diamond and Naomi hadn't talked in almost a month, and that was unusual. They each had a key to one another's place for emergencies, so Naomi pulled up to Diamond's place without prior notice. When Naomi pulled up, she noticed the Mercedes sitting in Diamond's driveway, but Diamond never mentioned to Naomi about getting a new car. She knew Diamond made money at the club, but she knew she didn't have it like that to be out copping a Benz and shit on a random day.

Naomi walked in, but the place was as quiet as a mouse. She searched around before heading upstairs to Diamond's bedroom. When she got upstairs, she found Diamond and Trill lying naked in the bed. Naomi hollered and banged on the wall to wake them.

"Get y'all asses up! Is this why I haven't heard from you lately and you haven't been to work in weeks?"

Naomi looked around the room from the door. "I guess you don't need the money now, huh?" Naomi continued after noticing all the jewelry on the dresser, the Coach handbags near the closet, and the Steve Madden, Louis Vuitton, and Dooney and Burke shopping bags stacked along the wall across the room. *This bitch living it up now,* Naomi said to herself.

"Close the fuckin' door! Let me get dressed, damn!" Diamond hollered.

"Ain't like I haven't seen yo' ass naked before. Shit, the whole city has. What makes it different now?" Naomi sighed.

Naomi slammed the door shut. Trill laid in the bed with the sheet across his private and his head propped up on several pillows. He didn't budge at all, leaving it up to Diamond to handle her girl. Diamond snatched one of his T-shirts to throw on and headed downstairs where Naomi was.

"What the fuck is wrong with you?" Diamond asked.

"Oh, what's wrong with me? Ain't shit wrong with me. What the hell has gotten into you? You don't answer my calls anymore, and you don't come to work anymore. Damn, what's going on? So you're head over heels for this nigga now?"

Naomi pointed upstairs where he was.

Naomi continued. "The same dude you said you didn't want and just wanted to finesse? He done swaddled you in with some dick and some money, now you're all up his ass?"

"Damn, shut up! Just listen to me. We are dealin' now, but we've been taking things slow. You was right; he's gonna take care of me."

"Dealin?" Naomi asked.

"Shhh, keep it down. He's the shit, girl. I'm glad you talked me into going out with him. Since then, he has been paying my bills and giving me lots of money. With how much he's giving me, I don't need to go to the club anymore. Did you see the car he bought me?"

"So that's your car?"

"Yes, girl. I finally got rid of that raggedy ass Camry you've been complaining about. And guess what? He paid it all cash."

"Damn, so he has money like that?"

"Yes, bitch! That's what I'm saying. Why do I need to go to the club now? He pays me without going there. He was my biggest paying client anyways. I never planned to make the club a permanent thing, but

79

I didn't know I would be able to get out so soon. I can't pass up this opportunity."

"How long have y'all been *in a relationship*?" Naomi asked her.

"Three and a half weeks now." Diamond bragged.

"Diamond, so you're telling me he bought you a car, fancy purses, designer shoes and shit… all in three weeks?"

"No. He's been buying me things since we went out on the date."

"What have you been doing for all of this before then? I know he ain't that kindhearted."

"Nothing. Well, just the same thing I did for him at the club… and a little more. You know what, don't worry about it!"

"A little more? Like what?" Naomi whispered.

"Don't worry about it!" Diamond said as she walked off from Naomi into the kitchen. Naomi got up from the coffee table where she sat and followed. On her way there, she saw men shoes and a few pieces of men clothes lying across the sofa.

"Are these his too?"

"Yeah, why?"

"So this nigga lives here now?"

"Hell no. He told me he has his own place, but he sleeps here sometimes. I haven't been over to his place yet, but he told me he will take me soon," Diamond explained.

Naomi shook her head from side to side.

"You better be careful. I've seen shit like this before. You are head over heels, and you hardly know this nigga; you better be careful. I'm here if you need me, but I'm heading out. I gotta go."

"It's not even like that, but I'll call you."

"Uh huh," Naomi said, not believing anything Diamond told her.

Diamond went back upstairs, not thinking much about how Naomi felt or what she said to her. She walked into the room to Trill completely naked, showing off his fine ass body and how much he wanted hers.

"What are you doing, silly? I just gave you some a couple hours ago," she told him.

She was playing hard to get, but she still wanted more. She lifted the t-shirt she had on, showing him that she was still naked underneath. She eased her body on top of his. He ran his fingers across her back, moving from her neck down to her waist. It didn't take long before Trill felt her juices dripping on the tip of his dick and slid himself inside of her. He always had to force himself in because her tightly gripped pussy didn't make it easy.

"Uh, shit! You got some good twat, girl! You know that, don't you?"

"Mmhmm," Diamond moaned.

"I can't get enough of you, Diamond. I love this shit," he said to her in between the sound of her clapping cheeks.

"This is your pussy, Trill!" Diamond hollered.

He slapped her ass and told her, "Say it again."

"This your pussy, Trill!"

He slapped her ass and pounded her pussy harder, making her juices splatter all over the sheets.

"Louder!" he hollered.

She screamed at the top of her lungs one last time, and his thick gooey cum was covering her a few minutes later.

Chapter 7
"Take it Slow"

The next week, Diamond went to get the boys. It'd been a month since she saw them and was keeping them for the weekend. She felt awkward pulling up in the car she never thought she'd be able to afford, in the projects she struggled in, but it felt damn good to her. She had a surprise for Ms. Mable as well, for all the help she'd been giving her with the twins.

When Diamond pulled up, Ms. Mable was sitting outside her door, watching the boys play in the field she called a backyard. When the twins ran up to Diamond yelling, "Mommy, Mommy!" Ms. Mable looked up over her glasses.

"Is that your new car?" Jordan asked.

Diamond looked back at the car and said, "Yes, baby. It's our new car. We don't have to drive that old beat up one anymore. I don't have to fight this one in order for it to work."

She loved how enthused the boys were to see her, but most importantly being able to explain to them that she was working hard on providing better days for them. They were getting older and understanding more, which was the reason she was pushing for change so quickly.

"How have y'all been doing over here? Have y'all been taking care of Ms. Mable?" she asked the twins.

"Yeah, but we are ready to come home. It's scary over here," Jordan said.

"What do you mean?" Diamond asked.

"We hear people fussing all the time, and we heard gunshots the other day," Josh answered.

A few of the tears she'd been holding back escaped her eyes, so Diamond turned her head to hide them. She began to have flashbacks from the moments she had on that very block as a kid. She rubbed her forearm across her face.

"Mommy? Are you OK? We didn't want to make you sad."

Diamond started sniffling.

"Aren't y'all the sweetest. Mommy's fine. We all are going home together," she told them, smiling.

"Today?" the twins asked.

"Yes, today! Give me hugs and kisses." They both ran into her arms, giving her hugs and kisses as she requested.

"Now go on and play. Let me talk to Ms. Mable for a second," she continued.

Diamond leaned down to Ms. Mable and kissed her on the forehead. Diamond watched her hands move quickly with the crochet.

"So, I see you are still making blankets for the homeless."

"Yep! Ain't nothin' changed around here except you pulling up in that expensive car. Now I'm no fool, Diamond. I know you doing something other than bartending. You are a grown woman, and I hate to question you, but if I'm going to be helping you out with these boys, I ought to know the truth. Ain't no way in hell you can afford that car so quickly."

"I am bartending like I told you. I also have this guy friend who's been helping me out and gifted me with the car."

Ms. Mable groaned and glanced up at her again. "It is a nice car."

"How have the kids been around here with you and in school?"

"They were good as usual. Those kids are never a problem for me. It's these ones with no home training that I have to worry about. Those kids missed you. They've been asking about you all the time. I know you call, but that's not enough for those babies. They want to be home with you."

"I know. I'm not working as much now, so I'll be a full-time mommy again."

"Good for you. They would love that."

"I'm going to run to the bathroom really quick before we head out, OK?"

"Go on and do what you need to do," Ms. Mable told her.

While in the bathroom, she reached in her purse and ripped off a piece of paper off an envelope she had. She wrote a note that read:

Ms. Mable, I don't know what the boys and I would do without you. You've been a tremendous help and loved on us like your own. I left you $8,100 to be exact. Please take this money and get out of the hood. You've been here long enough, and I want better for you. If you need help with anything, let me know.

We love you,

Signed, Diamond

As soon as she opened the bathroom door, she poked her head out to make sure Ms. Mable was still sitting outside. Since she was, Diamond walked in her room, placed the note and the cash on the wooden stand that set next to her bed, then quickly left out before getting caught. She knew if Ms. Mable saw it before she left, she wouldn't accept it. She always mentioned to Diamond that she wasn't looking for anything in return from her because she knew how much God would bless her.

"Alright, we are gonna get going. Come on, boys. Give Ms. Mable one last hug so we can go."

The boys got excited. Not only to be going home, but Diamond had been buying them things nonstop since she had more money now. They ran straight to their rooms when they got to the house, hoping to find more toys, video games, clothes, shoes, or even money, but it looked the same as it did before they left.

Diamond stood in the hallway with her hands on her hips, watching them.

"It's nothing different in there. The surprise should be here in a minute."

Since Diamond and Trill were official now, she thought it was important for the boys to meet him. He was good to her, and she couldn't wait to see how he interacted with the twins. She knew for sure it would be something the boys would be excited about since they hardly had a male figure around. They would have someone they could be rough with, play sports with, and hang out with instead of being under women all the time.

"What is it? What is it?"

"I'm not telling. You'll have to wait to find out."

Moments later, the doorbell rang. Diamond got up to open the door and yelled "surprise!" as she turned around and looked at the boys. They sat on the couch stumped.

"Who's that?" Josh asked.

"This is—" Diamond began to explain, but Trill cut her off.

"What's up, little man? You can call me Tee"

"Mr. Tee," Diamond chimed in.

Jordan dapped Trill while Josh sat on the couch with no interest in getting to know him at all. Trill walked over to him and asked, "What's your name?" but Josh didn't say a word.

"My momma told me not to talk to strangers," Josh said.

"Stop being rude!" Diamond hollered. She walked closer to him, snatched him by the arm, and pulled him outside on the porch so she could talk to him.

"What the hell is your problem? When an adult asks you a question, you answer. Do you understand me?"

"Yeah."

"Yeah? It's yes, ma'am. Where are your manners?" Diamond asked.

"Yes, ma'am."

"That's more like it."

"Who is he, Ma?" Josh asked.

"It doesn't matter who he is to me. He's an adult to you, and you need to treat him as such. I know your father hasn't been around, your uncle left us a few years ago, and you're still hurting, but you need to chill. All of that has been hard for me as well. I'm learning to cope with it day by day, and even though Uncle Rod has been gone for three years now, it's still not easy. Mr. Tee can be the father figure to you that you never had. He's gonna be around, so give him a chance."

"OK, but I don't know him."

"Well, that's OK. You'll have time to get to know him."

"I don't feel comfortable around him like I am with Ms. Mable and Auntie MiMi."

"It's gonna be fine. He's a good person. He's been doing nice things for me and for y'all. He got us this nice car. It's reliable and pretty. It's something I've always wanted. He bought y'all new beds. He buys me shoes and purses and gives me money. He's a really good guy. Can you be nice and give him a shot at this… for me?"

"I guess I can. Anything for you, Ma."

Diamond kissed Josh on the forehead and hugged him, holding him tightly.

"Thank you, baby. Now come on. Let's go back inside."

They walked back into the house to Trill and Jordan sitting on the floor playing with Hot Wheels. Josh walked over to Trill and introduced himself, playing nice as he promised his mom he would.

"Who wants to go shopping for new toys and video games?" Trill asked, jumping up from the floor.

"Me! Me! Me!" Jordan hollered excitedly.

"Only if your mom is up for it," Trill said.

Diamond smiled and said, "Sure."

"What about you, little man?" Trill asked Josh.

Josh looked at his mom. "Me too," he told Trill.

Trill laughed. He knew Josh would be a handful, but a five-year-old didn't scare him. Jordan took off running to the cars, and Josh ran behind him.

"I'm sorry about Josh. His dad has been absent all his life. He isn't used to having a man around."

"Little man is good. Kids love me. Just give him some time."

"Thank you, baby. You are so understanding," Diamond told him, sneaking a kiss before the boys saw them.

Trill ran behind the boys and hollered, "So do y'all wanna take mommy's fancy girly car, or do y'all wanna ride in my fast Ferrari?"

"Ferrari," the twins said at the same time.

"Then the Ferrari it is," Trill told them.

He knew he was coming over to meet Diamond's boys, so he had plans already to take them to the store. He knew if he wanted to keep Diamond around, he had to win her kids over too. He knew how much his kids loved riding in his Ferrari, so he drove that car instead. Little did Diamond know, him pretending to like the kids and be around them was all a front. She was blind to so many things he was doing to have the completed family she always wanted.

All she wanted was love, peace, and happiness. Trill gave her butterflies when she was around him. He made her smile like no man had ever made her smile before. And he showed her a life she knew she wanted but never thought she would have. Look at this bitch, booed up like she said she wouldn't be, but she couldn't ignore the effect he had on her mind, her body, and her heart. Here she was, falling in love over the things he did to and for her, instead of how his heart really felt.

Chapter 8

"Welcome to the Trap"

A week went past, and after spending lots of time together, she stressed to Trill how badly she wanted to go to his place, so he agreed to take her. Diamond was excited to see where he spent most of his time when he wasn't over at her house. She knew he had something nice and fancy that she could brag to Naomi about. She couldn't wait to see what he called his home.

Sitting in the middle of a trap house for the first-time had almost blown Diamond's mind. When Trill mentioned that he was taking her to his place, she had no idea he was talking about this. She turned around constantly, looking over her shoulder because she was nervous as hell to be in such a place. All she saw was Trill sitting next to her with about 10lbs. of weed, a couple kilos of cocaine, and tons of money in front of him with the money counter not too far away.

Trill tricked Diamond into believing that he was going to take her, but the entire time, he knew he wasn't. He had secrets he hadn't told her, one of them being where he lived. He only revealed bits and pieces of the truth to her.

"What the fuck am I doing here?" she asked.

Trill could see that Diamond was starting to panic, so he tried calming her down.

"Chill. Just calm down, sweetheart."

Diamond sat beside him, looking at him periodically as she tried to understand what the fuck was going on around her. It was her first time there, hoping that it would be her last. Nothing about that place was settling for her. Especially when all she could think about was how much trouble she would be in if that day was the day the place got raided.

She watched Trill as he leaned over the table in front of him. He cut open a kilo to bag separately. In the process, he rolled up a loose hundred-dollar bill he had near him and dipped one end in the line of coke. Right before Diamond's eyes, she saw him snorting the coke just before hitting a burning blunt. She didn't know what else to do except sit there and watch.

"I don't need to be here. Why am I here?"

"You are my girl, right?"

"Yeah…"

"OK then."

"You aren't nervous about me being here after knowing me for just four and a half months?"

"Nope! You won't open your mouth about this either, 'cause if you do, I'll blow your fuckin' brains out."

Trill took his gun out of his pants and held it to Diamond's head. She started shaking nervously, hoping he wasn't about to pull the trigger.

"Pow," he said, implementing what he would do to her if she double crossed him. He started laughing after seeing how scared she got. He took a few more puffs off the blunt and scooted the white over to her.

"Uh uh. Hell no! I'm not doing that shit. No way in hell. My life ain't that bad off, my nigga. I'm not wit' this shit. I'm not a fuckin' cokehead," Diamond quickly said.

Trill got up and stood in front of Diamond, leaning in toward her. He rubbed his nose then took two more puffs off the blunt. He blew the smoke directly in her face.

"So what are you trying to say, that I'm a fuckin' cokehead?"

Diamond coughed from all the smoke that depleted her lungs.

"I hope not. I damn sure ain't sticking by one either."

Trill had his fingernails dug deeply in Diamond's face before she could blink her eyes. He held her face tightly, where she couldn't move at all. He shoved the blunt between her lips and insisted that she inhaled. Diamond started coughing hysterically, but he still held the blunt between her lips. Finally, Diamond got the concept of it and smoked the rest of it smoothly.

"How do you feel?" Trill asked.

Diamond sat in the chair, rolling her tongue constantly, trying to understand why her mouth got dry suddenly. She laughed uncontrollably about any and everything, and she talked nonstop. Not to mention, she was paranoid as hell and on high alert with her surroundings.

"I feel weird, and my mouth is dry," she told Trill.

He laughed and said, "It's called cotton mouth. You'll get used to it."

She sat back down in the chair.

"Why did you make me do this?" she asked.

"'Cause, this shit eases your mind. You're too fuckin' uptight all the time. You needed to chill out, and I had the perfect thing to help you with that. This is some gas right here, the best thing on the market, and because you fuck with the plug, you just got this shit for free."

"The plug?" she asked. She was illiterate to the street code and what he meant. She'd never been around anyone who was in the streets like he was. His dialect was foreign to her, as if he spoke a different language.

"This shit is illegal. I don't want to be involved in any of this. I can't go to jail for anybody. I'll go back to the club and make my money the legal way if I have to. I don't want any part in this." Diamond continued.

Trill jumped up from his seat and started slapping everything off the table onto the floor. Diamond got scared and balled up in her seat. He walked over to her, and before she could say anything, the palm of his hand met the right side of her face.

She was astonished by what happened. She held the side of her face as the tears rolled down her cheeks. Not taking her eyes off of him for one second, she sat and thought heavily about what she said that was so bad for it to trigger him to hit her. She never thought he would put his hands on her. Now she was fearful, not knowing what he would do next. He paced back and forth in the room as he boxed the walls.

He went back over to her and snatched her face so hard she had no choice but to sit upright and face him directly.

"Don't ever mention going to that motherfuckin' club again. That shit is over and done with. No bitch of mine will be in a fuckin' club getting naked in front of other men! Do you know how that would make me look? I take care of you! Don't you ever... ever mention that fuckin' club again! Do you understand?"

Without hesitation, Diamond nodded her head up and down as hard as she could, but she didn't have much control of her head since it still sat in his hands.

"Good! Oh, and another thing, you won't be going anywhere. You are already involved, and you better not tell anyone about my organization, not even that bitch from the club that you hang with. As a matter of fact, you won't be chillin' or talkin' to her ass anymore either! I don't need any bad influences around my baby girl."

"But... she's not a bad influence, she's my—" Diamond started to say, but Trill went back over to her and slapped her on the right side of her face again.

"And don't be talking back! Do you hear me, bitch? There's a lot of changes to be made around this motherfucker! I see your mouth is gonna get you in a lot of trouble."

Diamond continued to cry. She was shaken up about everything that he did and said to her. She thought about the last conversation her and Naomi had but realized it was too late for her to listen. Being with Trill and seeing who he was, had her in a fucked-up place.

He went over to where he sat previously and reached down on the floor where he knocked the drugs off of the table.

"Damn! Look what you made me do; you made me waste my product on the damn floor."

Trill reached in his pocket for two bills and folded each of them a couple times. He scraped some coke off the floor with one of the folded bills onto the other. With the same hundred-dollar bill he had rolled up, he snorted more coke. He got up and went over to Diamond. He held the coke to her face, and with the other hand, he put the rolled-up bill to her nose.

Diamond started shaking her head side to side constantly as she began to cry again.

"I can't… I can't do this… Please don't make me… Please, I'm begging you."

Trill flared out his nose and lifted his hand up to her again, as if he was going to hit her once more.

"What the fuck did I tell you about talking back!" he hollered.

"I don't know how… please."

"Just close one nostril and slowly inhale, not too hard. It's going to make you feel better, baby girl."

Diamond looked at him hesitantly, but she knew she didn't have a choice. Although it killed her inside, she did as she was told. It burned her nose, but she continued without complaining because she didn't want to get hit again.

Just moments after the coke got into her system, she felt something running along her face, but she was still high off the weed, so didn't think anything of it. Then she felt liquid on her chest and realized she was sweating heavily. She knew she wasn't hot at all, so she started to panic, and her hands started shaking uncontrollably.

"What is going on?" she asked Trill.

"It's your first time. This is normal," Trill said, brushing off everything that was happening to her. When he got up to go to the bathroom, he looked at Diamond.

"Uh shit."

"What's going on? What? What?" Diamond panicked.

Before Trill could tell her, Diamond felt a drip of liquid on her lip. She thought it was sweat, but when she looked at her finger, she saw red.

"Oh my God! I'm bleeding! What's going on?" she continued to ask.

"It's just a nosebleed. You ain't dying. Come on to the bathroom so you can clean yourself up. We can go back to the house when you are done."

Trill went into the bathroom to pee while Diamond followed behind him to clean herself up. Her new MK shirt was ruined with blood covered all over the front, and for some reason, that was what she cared more about. She stood in the mirror cleaning her nose as she tried not to focus on how bruised the side of her face was. She couldn't help but to turn her head and move in closer to get a better look.

With the overload of the weed and coke high together, she began to get nauseous. She took in more than her body could handle, for just a first-time user. She vomited in the sink and hit the floor right after.

Trill dropped beside her on the floor. "Baby girl? Baby girl?" He called her name multiple times, but she was unresponsive. He knew he couldn't call 911 because of where he was and what he had inside. The last thing he wanted was to get all his money and product confiscated and sit in a cell from sunup to sundown over a bitch he wasn't sure would be around long term. Instead, he thought logically on how he could better this situation by himself.

He took off one of his t-shirts and ran it under the cold faucet and placed it over her forehead. *Damn, she hit the floor pretty hard. I hope she doesn't have a concussion or some shit,* he thought to himself. He went to the fridge and got a few bottles of cold water. He opened a bottle and poured it on her face directly. By the time the bottle was gone and he was opening another, she started coughing.

"What happened?" she asked.

"Nothing. Just drink this water. Don't stop. I want you to keep drinking it until all is gone."

When she was done downing the bottled water, Trill helped her up from the floor and into the car. He locked the trap up and made a few phone calls to his workers to take over what he couldn't finish.

What Diamond didn't know was she wasn't the only one that Trill laid hands on. He abused all of his women, even Treasure.

They drove home in complete silence. He was guilty of how he treated her but didn't let that stop him from checking on her. Diamond didn't say much. Although it was dark, she looked out the window the entire ride home. Just when they got around the corner from the house, Trill noticed blue lights in the rear-view mirror.

Diamond got nervous because she knew what Trill was into, and she now had illegal drugs in her system. Trill quickly took his gun off his hip and put it underneath the driver's seat. He threw on his seat belt and told Diamond to act normal.

"I know you are high, but try not to show them that. I'll do all the talking and handle everything. Just look out the window like you were."

A black police officer walked up to the driver's side, and Trill rolled down his window.

"May I ask what's the reason you are stopping me, Officer?"

The officer started laughing. He knew exactly who Trill was but seemed shocked to see Diamond sitting beside him.

"License and registration, please."

"You still haven't told me why you stopped me," Trill responded.

"Motherfucker, I said license and registration, please. You don't wanna make this difficult, I promise you."

Trill mumbled underneath his breath, "Oh, I don't," as he reached by Diamond to get the requested documents out of the glove box. He handed them over to the officer. The cop stood by the car window and looked at the paperwork Trill gave him. Trill already knew what was going on. He got fucked with by the police a lot for all the flashy things he had and the stereotype of a dope dealer he carried.

The officer leaned in the driver window as if he wasn't an officer on duty but a prostitute instead. "Terrell Austin, or should I call you Trill? I know about you."

Diamond threw her neck to the left, looking in the direction of the police wondering how the hell he knew who he was and if he thought she was suspect as well. Before Trill could speak, the officer continued.

"Don't I know you?" he asked Diamond.

"I'm afraid not," she responded quickly.

"Yeah, don't you work at that strip club? I've seen you a few times, and you do a damn good job."

Trill began to get upset. He looked at Diamond in her face then down to where the blood was on the front of her shirt. Diamond followed Trill's eyes and immediately covered it with her arm.

"She doesn't work there anymore. Man, listen, what are we doing because I have shit to do!"

"Can you let the young lady speak for herself?" the cop asked Trill.

The officer walked over to Diamond's window and tapped on it a few times for her to roll it down.

"What happened to your face? Are you OK?" he asked her.

"Brah, she's good. What are we doing? I said we have shit to do. Now are you giving me a ticket or something or just stopping me to be an asshole like how all you crooked ass cops do?"

The officer tossed Trill's license and registration back to him.

"This won't be the last time we see each other!" He hollered across Diamond at Trill then winked at him.

"Bitch ass cop." Trill mumbled underneath his breath and pulled off.

Chapter 9

"Watch ya hands"

As Diamond laid in the bed still, she stretched and yawned. She was suddenly waking from one of the best sleeps she'd had in days. She couldn't ignore all the ruckus she heard going on downstairs though. It sounded like slamming as if the twins were playing rough.

"Boys, quiet down. It's too early for all that noise!" she hollered.

Almost immediately after she finished yelling, they both came running in the room to her, but she still heard noise.

Diamond got up from the bed, curious to know what was going on. *If it's not them, then what the hell is all this noise?* she asked herself.

She slid her feet into her fluffy Dolce and Gabbana slippers then threw the matching robe on around her and headed downstairs. She was still half sleep, but that didn't stop her from going to see what the hell was going on.

As she approached the noise, she held on to the railing, making sure that she didn't go stumbling. She didn't make it down the stairs completely before she stopped. Diamond always kept her place cleaned, so for her to see what her living room looked like maddened her. Her living room and dining room floor was covered in boxes that Trill brought. So many were there, she could hardly see the floor or even walk through. It was a damn mess.

Diamond could tell what was happening and she was bothered, but she didn't know how to express her feelings to him after he put his hands on her for the first time at the trap house last week. That was something she never wanted to experience again, but she also wanted to know the answer to just one question and one question only, so she asked.

"Why is all of this in here?"

"Baby, I gotta move in for a while," Trill said.

Diamond was stunned. She came down the stairs completely and tiptoed in the tight empty floor space she did have.

"Why? You still aren't telling me anything. You said you had your own place, and now all your things are here. Did you get evicted? Was the place robbed? What happened? I need to know."

Trill was moving boxes and breathing heavily from exhaustion.

"Listen, don't worry about it. I'll explain later. I've been taking care of your bills anyways, so what's the problem?"

Diamond looked around at all the boxes, all his clothes that were thrown across her sofa and loveseat. She glanced over to all his shoes that were lined neatly along the walls. She looked over to the pictures of his kids he had scattered across the coffee table, but she didn't say much. If she did, she knew it would only cause more confrontation, so she bit her tongue instead and walked away.

"Of course, it's not a problem."

Diamond started walking upstairs and hollered to Trill. "I'll be upstairs if you need me!"

She walked past the twins' room, stuck her head inside their door and whispered to them to get dressed. She went in her bedroom and closed her room door behind her, preparing herself for a day out with her kids. She was in the mirror doing her hair and makeup when Trill came bursting through the room door. The sudden noise startled her, especially since he was calm with her when she stood downstairs with him just ten minutes before.

"What is your problem? Why did you come busting through the door like that?" she asked.

Trill didn't say anything. Instead, he walked toward her, giving her a devious look. When he got closer to her, she noticed the white residue around the base of one nostril. She already knew what he'd done, so she tried keeping calm as their conversation continued. She wanted to get out of the house with her boys in peace before things got out of hand.

"So... so it's a problem that I moved in, but it wasn't a problem for me to pay your bills?"

"Trill, what are you talking about? I never said it was an issue."

"You had an attitude when you saw the boxes downstairs, so don't fuckin' lie to me, Diamond!"

"Listen, there is no issue, OK?"

"You're up here gettin' all sexy and shit! Where the hell do you think you are going?"

"Sexy? No! I'm spending the day with my boys, that's it. Let me ask, is it fine with you, since I need to ask you permission for everything?"

Trill grabbed Diamond by the hair and wrapped it around his hand twice. He snatched her quickly, knocking all her makeup on the floor, and dragged her to the bed. She hollered multiple times, demanding him to let her go, but Trill acted as if he never heard her.

"So you think I'm stupid now, don't you? You don't need to do your makeup to be out with your kids. I know you're dropping them off and going out with another nigga. I'm not stupid, Diamond. And you ain't going nowhere."

Diamond cried. "What are you talking about? Why are you doing this to me? I'm not cheating on you. I was wanting to have some fun with my kids. I promise that's it. We'll be back before you know it."

"I don't believe you."

Diamond continued to cry. "You're hurting me. Please let me go."

Trill slapped Diamond. This time, on the opposite side of her face from the first time.

"I've told you about talking back to me, but see, your little ass just won't listen."

Trill started pounding on Diamond's head constantly. She balled up at the foot of her bed, taking every blow. She cried and hollered loudly; that was all she could do. Every time he got on coke, he abused her. She knew that was one drug he couldn't go without and wasn't going to. She knew if she left him, she would have nothing. If she called the cops, it would only make things worse. She felt helpless. She didn't know what to do, but she knew she couldn't keep taking the abuse from him.

Diamond's room door was wide open. The boys heard all the commotion and their mother crying out for help. They ran in to rescue her. Jordan tried pulling his mom away from Trill, while Josh tugged on Trill's arm, pulling him in the opposite direction.

As the boys pulled on each of them, it made Trill angrier. At that point, his focus was no longer on Diamond. Trill snatched his arm loose and boxed Josh on the left side of his forehead. Josh cried as he held his head, staring at his mom that was no help to him. Before Josh knew it, Trill had his back pinned to the wall with nowhere for him to turn.

"Stay out of grown folks' business, you hear?"

Josh balled up his mouth just before saying to Trill, "You ain't my daddy. Get off of me! Leave me and my mama alone."

"Just let my baby go. Please, Trill, he's just a kid." Diamond cried.

Trill never responded to Diamond, but after a few minutes, he turned Josh loose. Josh was still upset. He stood in front of Trill, breathing heavily, with both of his fists balled up, his eyebrows wrinkled, and one side of his lip lifted.

Diamond got up from the floor slowly. She walked over to Josh with all intentions to get him away from Trill before things got worse. Trill stood in front of Josh and laughed in his face.

"What you gone do, lil' nigga? You can't beat me." Trill continued to laugh.

Diamond grabbed him. "Come on, baby. Just calm down. Let's go to your room." He snatched away quickly from her. She never realized how strong he was for just a five-year-old until then.

"Yeah, lil' man, listen to yo' mama. Carry ya little ass on to your room."

Diamond pulled Jordan out of the room. She wrapped her arms around them both. "Come on, boys. I'm so sorry about all of this. Everything will get better soon. I will fix this, I promise," she whispered.

Jordan nodded his head, and Josh looked at Diamond in disappointment from her not helping him.

"Can we just go back to Ms. Mable's? It's not safe there either, but I'd rather be with her than here," Jordan asked.

Diamond felt a shiver through her body with disbelief in what she heard. She missed her boys so much and was excited about bringing them home to a better life. She knew it wasn't safe for any of them to be around Trill, but she never wanted to hear anything like that from her kids. Neither did she want them feeling this way in their own home, something she worked hard to provide for them and not Trill.

"No, baby. No! I need y'all here with me. I don't want y'all to go." Diamond cried.

"Mama, come with us. You can't stay here either. What if next time he hurts you badly?"

Diamond's eyes watered. She blinked many times to stop the tears from dropping, but she couldn't hold them back any longer.

Jordan wiped Diamond's tears with the back of his hand.

"Don't cry, Mama. We need to get out of here soon," Jordan reminded her.

"We will."

When Diamond noticed that Josh was still upset and he wasn't speaking much, she called him out about it.

"I know you're still upset, but talk to me."

Josh turned away from Diamond, and that's when she saw a massive knot on the side of his head, along with a few scratches.

Diamond wrapped her fingers around Josh's chin, turning his head more to get a better look. "Oh my! Baby, look at your face."

"Don't worry about it. I'll be OK," Josh finally said.

"Diamond? Diamond! Get your ass in here!" Trill hollered.

Josh sucked his teeth. She kissed each of them on the cheeks.

"I'll be back. Don't move. Stay in here, and keep the door locked and shut."

As Diamond walked down the hallway to the bedroom where Trill was, she smelled burning weed. She did like the feeling from the first blunt she smoked, but that was the only drug she was willing to use, and after how much stress she was under, she needed a puff or two.

She quickly walked to the room, and as soon as she got in there, Trill handed her the blunt. He sat at the foot of the bed, on the edge, and Diamond stood next to him while she hit the blunt a few times, just before passing it back to him.

When she was done, she went to sit on the opposite side of the bed. Diamond wasn't feeling him and was disappointed in his behavior lately. She thought a lot about Naomi and how much she regretted quitting the club. She wished she'd never left, because now, she couldn't move how she liked or do what she wanted now that she lived under Trill.

He crawled on the bed and threw his legs around her. He kissed on her neck, as if he didn't put hands on her and Josh just a half hour before. He expressed to her how sorry he was for the things he'd done. She wasn't upset with him for hitting her as much as she was for him hitting Josh. After she saw him in a rage and flip on her kid, that was her breaking point and knew she had to end things soon. Diamond knew there was only a matter of time before one of them got severely hurt by him.

"Come on, baby. Please don't be mad at me. I love you," he told her. He could tell from her body language and how quiet she was that he was in deep shit with her and skating on thin ice. Diamond frowned and rolled her eyes without him noticing. She knew he was full of shit, but with no job and no money, she needed his no-good ass to keep her and her kids off the streets. "I'm not feeling good. Is that different weed? Is it stronger or something?"

Trill smirked at her and said, "It's better."

"How do you mean better?" Diamond raised her voice. "What was that, Trill? What was it?" She panicked.

"It's weed—"

"And want else?" Diamond asked furiously.

"And coke."

"Damn it, Trill!" she hollered.

Diamond paced back and forth in the room with her hands on her head. "I knew I shouldn't have smoked that shit. What's up with you and coke lately?"

"Lately? Baby, I've been doing this. This shit ain't nothin' new to me. You need this shit too. Look how you be acting."

"No, I don't. I was fine before I did this. Before all of this," Diamond said, looking around the room, glancing in her closet at all her designer products, and then she looked at Trill.

"Girl, you are so ungrateful. Do you know how many bitches are all over my dick, dying for this life that I gave you?"

"I don't need any of this shit. I was better off without it, like I said. There's a lot of changes that needs to be made around here. I'm tired of being disrespected, mistreated, and left in the blind about things. I don't want to do these drugs with you anymore. I watched my mom do drugs as I grew up. I'm not going to end up like her and put my kids through the same shit I went through. I love my kids more than anything in this world. I can go without a lot of things in life, but one thing I won't continue life without are my kids."

Chapter 10

"Don't do this to me"

A week went by. Luckily, the boys were out all week on spring break, so Josh's scars were able to heal some, which was one of Diamond's concerns. Diamond got the boys up and ready for school. She stood in the kitchen, making the twins a bowl of cereal each before she dropped them off to school. She could tell they were still upset about everything that happened. She couldn't apologize to them enough for Trill's behavior and the things he said to them.

"I know y'all are still a little upset from everything that happened, but I can promise you I'm working on change for us. Try to have a good day today."

She hugged and kissed them both on the forehead.

"I want y'all to know that I love y'all. Now hurry and eat your breakfast before y'all are late."

Diamond started cleaning the kitchen before heading out, then Trill walked down the stairs to where they were.

"Good morning, baby. What's for breakfast?"

"I didn't cook. I only made the boys some cereal." The kids weren't the only ones who held a grudge against him.

"I guess I have to get my own damn breakfast then, shit!"

"We are pressed for time; I couldn't make it this morning."

Diamond looked at her phone and realized it was time for them to head out.

"Come on, boys. Empty your bowls and grab your backpacks. It's time for us to leave."

The boys got up and dropped their bowls in the sink. Then they ran to the living room, threw their bags over their shoulders, and headed on the porch to wait for Diamond.

"I have to go. Be safe out there. When do you think you'll be back home?"

"Probably not until late; we have a lot of weight to move. Don't wait up for me."

***

When Diamond pulled up to the school, she told the boys she loved them and to have a good day. Jordan responded to her, but Josh didn't. Trill wasn't the only one he was upset with. While walking to class, the twins started talking.

"Why didn't you say anything back to Ma?" Jordan asked.

"Because… I'm still mad at her."

"OK. Well I guess I understand. How are you gonna cover that up though?" Jordan asked, pointing at Josh's forehead.

"I'm not."

"What if someone ask what happened to you?"

"So what? I'm gonna tell the truth."

"I don't think that's a good idea," Jordan said.

Josh stopped Jordan from moving forward.

"I wanna go back to Ms. Mable's, don't you?"

"…Yeah." Jordan hesitated.

Josh continued. "Yeah, we saw a lot of bad things happening, but at least she didn't beat on us or allowed anyone else to do it either. What's gonna happen to us if we don't leave? I'm scared of Mr. Tee."

"But we can't leave Ma with him alone. What if something happens to her?"

"She can come too. I'm sure Ms. Mable wouldn't mind." Before the twins parted ways to their classes, they said one last thing to each other.

"I love you, bro."

"I love you too. I still don't think any of this is a good idea."

"Good morning. Welcome back to school. I hope everyone had a good spring break," Josh's teacher told the class.

She walked around, greeting each student. When she did that, she noticed Josh wasn't acting himself then noticed the scratches and bruises he had on the left side of his face.

"Mr. Johnson, can I have a moment with you outside in the hall?"

Josh never said anything. Instead, he dropped his backpack in his seat and walked out the door into the hall like she asked.

"Your face is a mess. Is everything going OK at home?"

Josh put his head down, indecisive about if he wanted to tell her about what happened or not. His teacher grabbed his chin and lifted it with her hands. When she did, she saw tears rolling down his cheeks. Josh was always hard core, so for her to see him crying, she knew immediately something was wrong. She told him stay put while she went next door to ask another teacher to watch her class for her, then she walked Josh down to the guidance counselor's office.

"Come with me, sweetie."

"Where are we going?" Josh asked.

"Just to the guidance office, no worries," his teacher said.

When they got to the counselor's office, Josh's teacher set him down and left him to go back to her students. While Josh sat in the office, waiting for the counselor to get off the phone, he began to get more nervous. He tapped his feet constantly while he began to sweat.

"Mrs. Houston is concerned about you. What's going on at home?"

Josh didn't answer her question.

"It's OK. Take your time. It's our responsibility to assure that our students are safe at school while in our care and when they are home. If what happened to your face was caused by something you did, then say that, but if it wasn't, I need to know. Sweetie, I can only help you if you tell me what's going on."

"Will something bad happen to my mom if I tell you?"

"Hopefully not. Did she do this to you?"

"No… it wasn't her. It… it was her boyfriend."

"Explain to me what happened."

Josh didn't feel like he could trust her, but he couldn't change his mind now; he had already said too much.

"My mom and her boyfriend got into an argument about something stupid. My brother and I were in our room when we heard it and we went to help her. When we did, I got hit in the process. I was just trying to help my mom."

"It's OK. Does he live at home with you?"

"Yeah. Now he does."

"Is there anyone else you could stay with until we straighten things out with your mom?"

"My auntie MiMi and this old lady named Ms. Mable who used to watch us all the time, but I don't think my mom want any of them in her business."

Josh sniffled and wiped his eyes with the sleeve of his sweatshirt then continued. "We will be OK. Just forget it. My mom says she have it under control. I don't know why I came here in the first place. Just don't tell my mom I told you."

"What will she do to you if she found out?"

"Nothing, but like I said, she doesn't want anyone in her business."

"Thank you so much, Mr. Johnson. I'm going to call your brother down to talk to him about all of this as well. Just have a seat outside my door for me."

Josh got up and did as he was told. A few minutes later, Jordan walked in and went past Josh into the office.

"Hi, Jordan. I am Ms. Fernando, the guidance counselor. You are not in trouble at all, but I called you down because I wanted your side of the story about what happened at home with your brother. Do you mind sharing that information with me?"

Jordan was frightened. He did not know what to say because him and Josh never talked about what to tell anyone if they asked. He didn't want to get anyone in trouble, so he refused to give the guidance counselor any information.

"I… I didn't see or hear anything. I don't know what happened." Jordan lied.

Ms. Fernando locked her fingers together and placed her hands on top of her desk. She leaned in a little more toward him so she could look him deeply in the eyes.

"Just be honest with me, kid. You won't get in trouble. Ensuring that our students are safe here and at home is our priority. I have already gotten your brother's side of the story, so tell me. Tell me what happened at home."

"This really didn't have anything to do with my mom."

"Your mom will be fine. I can't help unless I know what happened."

Ms. Fernando finally got Jordan to crack. He confirmed what his brother told her happened in the room. "What did your mom do?"

"She didn't do anything except holler at Mr. Tee. That's all she could do. I think she's afraid of him."

"Does he beat her all the time?"

"I don't know. We are at Ms. Mable's a lot; that was the first time we saw it happen."

"What about you? Has he hit you before?"

"No… no, ma'am.

"Does he live at home with you all?"

"Now he does."

"Do you have a number for Ms. Mable?"

"No, my mom has her number."

"Thank you so much, Jordan. We will do all that we can to get this situation all figured out. None of our students should feel unsafe at home, let alone be abused. Have a seat outside the door with your brother for me. I'm going to call your mom."

Jordan went out and sat next to Josh. Ms. Fernando closed the door behind him.

"What did she ask?" Josh whispered to Jordan.

"She only asked what happened."

"And what did you tell her?"

"The truth. What else was I supposed to say? Man, I have a bad feeling about this," Jordan said.

"Did you tell her everything?"

"Yeah."

"Why?"

"Because you told me to."

"I never told you to tell everything. I told you follow my lead."

"And what was that because you never made it clear what the plan was in the first place. All you said was you wanted to go back to Ms. Mable's."

"Bro…" Josh said.

"She's calling Ma."

"What? No! I told her Ma didn't want people in her business. Now we are gonna be in big trouble. You just made things worse," Josh told him.

Ms. Fernando opened her room door, and the boys got quiet.

She stood in front of them and said, "Don't worry. Everything will be fine."

They sat for almost an hour, then they saw Diamond walking quickly through the doors. She saw the boys and ran up to them, hugging and kissing them, concerned that they were hurt by the phone call she got.

"Hi, I'm assuming you are Ms. Johnson. May I have a word with you?"

Diamond got concerned. She looked around, back and forth at the boys and at the counselor.

"Is everything OK?"

"That's our concern and the reason I called you in. Do you mind stepping in my office for me so we can discuss this matter further?"

"Sure."

"I am Ms. Fernando. Josh's teacher brought him to the office because she was concerned about his face—"

"Oh…"

"Yes. So do you mind telling me what's going on at home?"

"Oh, that isn't anything. These boys play rough all the time. As boys, they argue and fight quite often. Like typical boys do. Is that what you called me here for?"

"Is that your answer? I've spoke to the boys each, alone, and their stories matched up more than yours do. Is this the story you are sticking to?"

"It's not a story, it's the truth."

"OK then. I guess our conversation here is over. There is no need to continue."

As soon as Diamond got up to walk out, there was a knock on the door. Ms. Fernando opened the door to a young Caucasian woman with a badge attached to her sweater and a clipboard in her hand. Diamond walked through the door past the woman without acknowledging her.

"Not so fast, Ms. Johnson. There is one other person I'd like you to meet," Ms. Fernando told her.

The boys were looking at each of them back and forth. They were trying to figure out why their mom seemed so upset and what was going on. They listened to every word said around them.

The Caucasian woman stuck her hand out and introduced herself to the boys.

"I'm Ms. Rodgers. It's my job to solve problems when kids are in similar situations like the one you are in. I know you may have heard this many times, but everything will be fine, I promise."

Ms. Rodgers stood up and turned to walk to Diamond, where she stood at a distance with her arms crossed.

"Ms. Johnson, I am Ms. Rodgers."

"Yeah, I heard you," Diamond said stubbornly.

"OK. Well, I am with child protective services."

Diamond got extremely upset once she said that. She knew what would happen next, and she couldn't believe she was in the predicament she was in.

"I'm not understanding what the hell that has to do with me and my kids. Everything is fine. I buss my ass as a single parent; they are all I have. I will not let y'all take them away from me."

"Ma'am, please calm down. I don't like to discuss things like this in front of the children. Can we go in Ms. Fernando's office?"

"Hell no! She probably was the bitch that called you."

"Making sure kids are safe at home is my job. From what we heard from them today, they are not safe at home with your boyfriend, and neither are you. We want to help you, but you have to allow us to do so," Ms. Rodgers told her.

"It ain't shit wrong with my household. Everything is fine."

"So, his face looks like that because everything is fine at home?" Ms. Fernando asked.

"Boys play rough. What's the fuckin' problem? Are you accusing me of hurting my kids? Is that what you are saying right now?"

"It may not be you, but it's somebody you know. Let me just say, grown men should not be putting hands on kids, resulting in something like that." Ms. Rodgers pointed in the direction of Josh.

Four police officers walked in the office where they were.

"Ms. Johnson, we have enough information to hold the kids in our custody. You will be contacted with a court date. At that time, the judge will decide what would be best for these kids. Thank you for your time," Ms. Rodgers said.

A police officer grabbed each of the boys and another grabbed Diamond.

"Mom!"

"Ma, what's going on?" Jordan cried.

"You can't take my kids away from me. You can't take my kids! Josh, Jordan, I love you both!" Diamond cried out.

"Ma?" Jordan cried, reaching his hands out to grab hers.

"Get off me! I want my mom!" Josh cried as he tried fighting them to get loose.

"You can't take them from me! They are all I have. Please! Please! Just let me and my boys go. They are all I have. Please don't take them from me!" Diamond continued.

Chapter 11

"Whatever it Takes"

Diamond cried her entire ride home. She didn't know what to do. The moment she got in the house, she ran upstairs to her room. She flipped over her mattress to get to the weed Trill hid underneath it. She never felt the need to smoke, unless he demanded that she do, but she was depending on that high to ease her mind. She was stressed out. She didn't have anyone to talk to. She wasn't allowed to talk to Naomi anymore, and there was no way in hell she could tell Ms. Mable what happened to the boys. Ms. Mable wasn't in the best shape with her health, and the last thing Diamond wanted was to kill her faster than she was already going.

Diamond didn't know shit about rolling a blunt because she never had to. She'd watched Trill many times, so she applied what she saw to do the best that she could. It wasn't the best looking, but the motherfucker burned and got her high, which was all that mattered. She lay across her bed, looking at the blank ceiling as she pulled on her blunt.

The thoughts constantly rolled through her head about how all of this was Trill's fault, how she wished she could change everything that happened, and how she couldn't wait to get her boys back home with her.

Since Trill wasn't home, she picked up her phone and called Naomi.

"Naomi, it's good to hear from you." Diamond cried.

"What's wrong?"

"I have to tell you something really bad."

"What? What's going on?" Naomi asked.

"It's about the boys."

"Tell me, Diamond. What's wrong? Is everything OK?"

Diamond got really emotional when Naomi asked her that.

"No. They were taken from me."

"When? Who took them? Why? You know what, I'm coming over."

"No! No! Please don't!" Diamond hollered.

"Why not?" Naomi asked.

"Because Trill doesn't want me talking to you anymore, OK? He's not here so I snuck and called you. Don't call back once we hang up. I will have to call you when I can."

"What the fuck, Diamond? What do you have going on?"

"I don't know, Naomi. This is nothing I saw coming."

"I thought you said he didn't live there."

"He wasn't living here when you asked that. He just moved in a week ago. I can't believe it's been so long since we talked. So much has happened."

"Sounds like y'all are in a lot of trouble. If y'all need to come back to my place until things get back in order, you know y'all are welcome. And you can call me anytime and come by. I miss y'all. I really do. At one point, I thought I did something to you, but now I know that it wasn't me. Please let me help you. Where are the boys?"

Naomi continued, "Please, Diamond. I'm begging you."

"I'll let you know if I need you to help," Diamond told her.

"Diamond, what happened to the boys?"

"I have to go, Naomi. I'll have to tell you about that later. I'll call you when I can. I love you, girl. Bye."

Diamond heard the front door close, and she lay across the bed, looking at the ceiling as if she didn't disobey Trill. She watched Trill peep in the boys' room while he walked along the hallway to the bedroom.

"Where the hell are they? Did you take them to that old lady's house again?"

Diamond didn't say anything to him. She was already upset being that she felt like it was his fault all of this was happening. She wasn't in the mood to argue or fight, so she kept her mouth shut.

"OK then, I guess you aren't talking to me. It's OK. It's cool."

Trill headed in the bathroom to take a shower. The built-up anger in Diamond led her to jump out of bed and go after Trill. She started beating on him and yelled, "This is all your fault. Look what you caused! I can't believe you. I'll always hate you for this." Trill was confused.

He turned around and grabbed both of her wrists to stop her from hitting him anymore.

"Stop! Stop! What the hell are you talking about?"

"The boys aren't at Ms. Mable's house. They are gone!"

"How do you mean they are gone? What happened?"

"After I dropped them off to school, I got called to come back. The guidance counselor decided that she wanted to question me about Josh's head. You know, the knot you gave him the other day."

"They called child protective services on me, and they took my fuckin' kids! I don't know what to do now. She told me I would get a letter in the mail soon, but I don't wanna sit around and wait for a fuckin' letter. I want my damn kids back. All of this happened because you were high on your coke and had to hit him."

"Just calm down."

"That's easy for you to say. You don't know what it's like to watch your kids get pulled away, hearing them cry out for you and not be able to do a fuckin' thing about it!"

Diamond got up and ran downstairs to the kitchen with Trill following her.

"I don't know shit about the process either, but what I do know is you need a good lawyer, and it ain't gonna be cheap," Trill said.

Trill slapped the side of the fridge, scaring Diamond in the process. "Damn! Now I gotta kick out money for a motherfuckin' lawyer. Shit!"

"You're acting like this isn't your fault right now! What's the problem? Don't you have the money?"

"Not really. That's why I've been gone for so long in the days. Shit is lookin' bad on the streets. People ain't fuckin' with me like they used to."

"I'm going to get the money regardless. I'm going to get my kids back with your help or not. If that means I have to go back to the club and shake my ass for some dollars, then I'm gonna do that. Even if it means I have to sell the Benz and all the designer shit in the room, then I will. Not a damn thing will stop me from bringing them back home, and I mean it!"

Trill laughed. "You sound crazy as hell right now. You don't know shit! You could work every day and all night at that club and you still won't have enough money. I've told you, you ain't going back to the fuckin' club. If you do, I'm leaving your ass like I did Treasure. She's still at the club and still don't have shit. What will you do when you have to take care of you and the kids alone and pay bills by yourself again? You depend on that club way too much. Don't get ahead of yourself. What goes up, must come down. Don't fuck around and end up like Treasure."

"Well are you gonna get me the money or not?"

"We are gonna get the money together."

"What you mean? I'm not a drug dealer."

"Neither am I. We won't be dealing it; I need you to bring it in."

"What if I get caught? I really won't be able to get my kids back then, 'cause I'll be in prison."

"You said you will do whatever to get your kids back, so are you down or not?"

Diamond hesitated. "Yeah, I'm down…"

"You only have to do this for a week, and you'll have the money for your lawyer in a couple of days after that. I know you don't wanna do this, but at least you will have what you need and a lawyer worth spending on."

Diamond leaned on the counter with one hand underneath her chin. Yeah, she was scared as hell, but she was also a mother. A mother willing to do anything to see her kids again, so like any mother, she did what she had to do.

"I'm in," she told Trill.

He walked up behind her and pushed aside her long blonde hair to kiss her on the neck. "That's my girl." He whispered in her ear.

"What do I have to do?"

"Smuggle drugs," Trill told her.

"How? How am I supposed to do this without getting caught? I don't know anything about this."

"You will need to stuff it in your pussy. You will be taught. You won't be alone. Don't worry."

"Who am I gonna be with? Where are we going?"

"I know you won't take this lightly when I tell you."

"Tell me! I need to know."

"You and Treasure will be going to a few places, but the first stop is Mexico. She has done this before, so she's much more prepared. The first thing we need to do though is get you a passport."

"Treasure? Oh, hell no! Why is she involved? I never knew you were still fuckin' with her."

Diamond got really upset when Trill mentioned Treasure. Treasure was no friend to her, especially after they fought and the things she said to Diamond at the club. She knew Trill conversed with her and saw her from time to time since they had a kid together, but she didn't understand out of all the women in the world, why her. Diamond soon found out from Trill, that when they dated, she helped Trill with his operation.

Treasure knew a lot about what he did from dating him years ago. After he stopped fucking with her, she threatened to give him up to the cops and rat him out if he didn't give her what she wanted. So, in order to keep her happy, he was sleeping with her still, giving her hush money, and involved her in his business.

When he mentioned to Treasure the problems he was having, she immediately offered to help. Nothing had changed for her. She still wasn't bringing home enough money. She needed money just as bad as Diamond and Trill did. She knew when Trill was low on money, she was too. When he lacked the finer things, she did too. Because of that, she couldn't leave him hanging, because she knew she needed him.

Once Diamond found out everything about Treasure and Trill, she opted out of the deal.

"Nope, I'm not doing it! You can have some other chick go instead. If she's in, I'm out. I can't believe you have been fuckin' around wit' her ass when you are supposed to be my nigga. No wonder why she trips on every bitch you fuck with. I can't believe you want me to work with this bitch and I don't even like her ass."

"This shit ain't about y'all silly ass beef. This shit is about the money. If you can't grow up and do what the fuck you have to for your kids like you said you would, then maybe I need to take your advice and find somebody else."

"If she's in, I'm out," Diamond repeated.

Trill snatched Diamond by her hair after she started to walk off then grabbed her by the shirt and pushed her to the wall. Diamond was frightened and started to regret everything she said to him. She was almost certain that he would beat on her because of it. She closed her eyes and prepared herself for what was about to come next. Then she didn't feel anything; instead, she heard him yelling.

"Look at me! Look at me! You don't have a fuckin' choice. She will be in our lives regardless, whether you like it or not. So get over it!"

"OK. Just let me go," Diamond said.

"That's my baby. You're what you call a down ass chick, a ride or die bitch. As long as you have my back, I'll have yours. You don't have to worry."

Diamond replied, "I got your back, bae, I got you. We are in this shit together." Trill smiled.

"Now fire up," he told her.

***

While Diamond was alone with Treasure, she took the time to get Treasure's side of who Trill was and what he was like in their relationship.

"I know we didn't start off on a good foot, but I'm really a cool ass person," Diamond told her as they sat in the airport."

"Yeah, alright," Treasure brushed her off, showing little interest in squashing the beef between them.

"I've seen pictures of Neveah, she's so cute and he talks about her all the time."

"Yeah, I bet he does. He hasn't seen her much since he left the house though."

"How long has that been?"

"I kicked his ass out right before he moved in with you."

Diamond scrunched her eyebrows and frown her mouth once she realized that was the reason he was there. He never told her that he was living with her, she thought he had his own place.

"Mmm…is that right?"

"Yep! I'm glad his ass is gone. We argued and fought about a lot of shit. He knows I need him, so he did what he wanted to me, without giving a fuck about how much it would hurt me. Being able to call him my nigga wasn't worth, getting cheated on, lied to and abused damn near every day."

"But now, I don't have to worry. I told him since he wanted to cheat on me with you, you can have him, because we are done. He's your problem now." Treasure continued.

Chapter 12

"In a Bind"

The last two weeks were busy for Diamond. She got the job done that Trill asked her and Treasure to take care of, she found an amazing lawyer, and she was preparing herself for the day that she didn't look forward to—her first court hearing. She didn't know what to expect, who would be there, and what they would ask, but she was hoping to see her boys.

She left Trill behind and decided to go alone. Diamond walked into the courtroom a nervous wreck. Her hands were shaking uncontrollably, as she tapped her feet and sweated like she'd just finish a good round of sex with Trill. The chick couldn't keep calm.

When Diamond's case was being acknowledged, she got up and took the stand. She answered all the questions that were asked. She didn't answer all honestly, but she said what she thought they wanted to hear.

As soon as she thought it was over, the judge asked her to take a drug test. Diamond nearly broke down in tears right in front of the judge, knowing there was no way in hell she would pass it. What mattered most was that she didn't show them any signs of nervousness. So, she agreed to take the test. Her test was scheduled to be done in the next few days and her follow-up court date was a week later.

Bang! She hit her hand on the steering wheel immediately after getting in the car.

"Fuck!" Diamond hollered.

She calmed herself down and called Trill. If anyone knew what to do about passing a drug test, it was him.

"Baby, we have a problem. I need you to meet me at the house ASAP!"

"What the fuck is going on, Diamond? What's up?"

"Just meet me at the house."

She sped, running every yellow light she came up on and hardly stopped for the stop signs. She didn't give a damn about a cop; she was more concerned about what she could do for her current situation. When she got home, Trill wasn't there yet. She sat on the couch in complete silence, thinking about what she was gonna do and what would happen if things didn't pan out right.

Diamond heard a car pulling up. Hopping up from the sofa, she quickly walked to the door to see if it was Trill. When she saw that it was, she pushed the screen door open and ran to his car. Trill got out of the car and leaned back on it. He hugged Diamond tightly while she buried her face in his shirt, crying.

"What's the matter? Talk to me! What happened at court today? Do you need a new lawyer? What's up?"

Diamond looked up at Trill and started crying harder. "I have to take a drug test."

"Word?"

Diamond rapidly shook her head up and down.

"What am I supposed to do? I'm fucked! There is no way I will get my boys back home after they discover that I have marijuana and cocaine in my system. Now what? Tell me, what am I supposed to do now?"

Diamond dropped to the ground and continued to cry. He grabbed her by her arm and lifted her up to walk her in the house. He knew about something that could be done, but he knew she wouldn't be down for it. It was a risky move, but if it went smoothly, it would be worth it.

He sat her down on the chair and sat next to her.

"You have no choice but to go and take that drug test. If you refuse it, I don't know what will happen. But who said it has to be your piss? We can go get some artificial urine and use it for the test instead of your own."

"I don't know. I don't think it's a good idea. I'm scared, Trill."

If Diamond did that, it would only fix part of the problem. The other problem was the kids did not want to come back home with Diamond unless Trill was gone, but she didn't tell him that part. That left Diamond in a bind because Trill took care of everything that she didn't have the money for, including the roof over their heads.

So much problems were coming down on Diamond at once. She kept him around, not realizing he was the cause to many of them, and the amount of problems would continue to rise as long as he was around. She'd been warned about him by so many people but continued to ignore the signs that he was no good for her.

*****

Diamond knew Trill would flip out if he knew where she was headed, but the complications in her life left her no choice. She went to the club to talk to Red Man about getting her job back. The club was her only way of leaving Trill alone completely. Men loved her there, so she knew she could make the money like she used to in no time.

She knew what time the girls started to arrive, so she went by a little earlier. Thankfully, only Red Man was there.

"Diamond! It's good to see you again. You don't look as good as you used to. Is everything alright?"

Diamond shook her head. "No, everything is not OK. I need my job back. I promise it will be better this time."

"Hell no! Word on the streets is that you are fuckin' with psycho ass Trill. I know how he goes behind his women and I'm not trying to rub him the wrong way and bring problems to myself or my club."

"Please, Red Man. I need this job back. I'm begging you! Please. I need this money."

"I'm sorry, Diamond. I would love to have you back, but I can't. You should have never left. You fucked that up for yourself."

"I know, and I told you, I won't—"

"It's a no, Diamond," Red Man said sternly.

Diamond snatched her purse and stormed out of his office. On her way out, Naomi stopped her.

"Hey, girl," Naomi said.

Diamond lift her head from her phone because she recognized the voice.

"Oh, hey! What are you doing here so early?"

"I needed to grab something, but what's up? You hung up so fast the other day, I didn't get a chance to say bye."

"I'm sorry. No hard feelings. I have a lot going on."

"C'mon. Let's sit in my car and talk. I can tell you haven't been yourself lately and I miss my friend," Naomi told her.

"I really don't have that much time."

"I'm not accepting no for an answer," Naomi said.

She grabbed Diamond by the wrist and dragged her to her car.

Diamond didn't fight it because, truth was, she needed someone to vent to about everything, and she missed Naomi just as much as she missed her.

"I don't know where to begin. You would not believe all the shit I have been through," Diamond said.

"Why haven't you called me? I was waiting to hear back from you when you hung up on me."

"I know, but I've been occupied with other shit. You don't even know the half. This relationship with him turned out to be a disaster," Diamond said.

"Tell me what's going on. Please."

"So, it started out cool. He was really nice and sweet to me. He took me out, bought the car, bought me designer shoes and purses, and took me out to the finer restaurants. He was giving me the life I wanted, and I was loving it. I couldn't get enough of him spoiling me, and when I got in deeply, he started to change. He started physically abusing me, and he made me smoke weed and sniff coke. He even made me traffic drugs for him. I found out that he's still sleeping with Treasure to keep her happy because he doesn't want her to snitch to the police about everything that he has going on."

"You are on drugs now?"

Diamond put her head down in shame.

"I had no choice. If I don't do what he says, he beats me."

Diamond pulled her hair back to show Naomi the bruising on the side of her face.

"Oh no, Diamond! You can't be with him. You need to leave him *now*!"

"That's easier said than done. What am I supposed to do? I have no money, I can't get the job back here, and I'm not going back to fast food. It wasn't enough money. That's why I left in the first place. He pays my bills, he gives me money, he feeds me, Naomi, and he does so much more. I need him!"

"No you don't. That's what he wants you to think so you would never leave, and he has made you believe that. I'm always here for you and the boys, and there's always space at my place for y'all. I'll move someplace else if I have to so he doesn't know where we are and so that you feel safer."

"I can't do it. I'm scared. There is no telling what he would do to me… and you, if I did go along with your plan."

"Just go to the police, Diamond. Get a restraining order on him. He's scared of the cops. I'm sure he won't bother you so the cops don't bother him."

"He has people working for him. He sends other people to handle things for him too. Everyone knows I'm his girl. He has eyes on me at all times, probably even now. So many people are terrified of this man and what he would do to them. He knows so many people, and he would have them after us in no time. They won't let up until Trill is satisfied either."

You're looking at me crazy, but you don't understand. He is dangerous, especially when he is on coke." Diamond continued.

"It sounds like you're making excuses, but I hear you. The other day when we were on the phone, you said the boys were taken from you. Where are they?"

"CPS has them." Diamond cried.

"What happened?"

Diamond explained to Naomi what happened. As soon as she was done, she noticed Naomi's eyes watering.

"Now what? What's gonna happen? You are going to get them back, right?"

"To be honest, I don't know right now. I have to go back to court next week, but in a few days, I have to take a drug test."

"And you were on the weed and coke," Naomi stated.

"Right. I don't know what to do. This shit is fucked up, MiMi! Why me?

I have the money for the lawyer, but the boys don't want to come home unless he's gone. If I put him out, how will I afford my bills? I can't get evicted again."

The car got quiet. Naomi stared at Diamond. Naomi began to feel guilty. She was the one initiating her and Trill's relationship. It was all her idea for Diamond to fuck with him in the first place, but she never knew it would turn out like this. All she knew was he had money, something Diamond needed and wanted.

Naomi saw how desperate and in need of help Diamond was.

"I may have a solution to your problem," she told Diamond. "Remember that money I've been saving for my business so I could leave the club?"

"There is no way in hell I'm taking your money. You worked really hard for that."

"How about let's use it for a fresh start. Let's move out of town once you get the boys back. You won't have to worry about Trill and all of his bullshit."

"I don't know, Naomi. I would have to think about that."

"There isn't much you should have to think about with an offer like that, but OK. I guess I understand."

Diamond looked at her phone and realized that Trill would be getting home soon.

"Damn! I didn't realize what time it was."

Naomi rolled her eyes. "Let me guess. You have to get home?"

"Yes! I have to go."

Diamond hopped out the car and gave Naomi a quick hug. While Naomi was hugging her, she saw Red Man standing at the club door, staring at them.

"What the hell is he doing? Being all nosy and shit."

"Who?" Diamond asked. She was paranoid with thoughts that Naomi was talking about Trill.

"I'm talking about Red Man's ass. Nosy ass motherfucker."

"OK. Girl, I have to go."

"Call me sometime so I know the you're OK. Call me when you leave the house or when he leaves, just for a second even. I need to know that y'all are OK!" Naomi hollered.

"I will."

"Think about what I told you!" She hollered at Diamond more while Diamond started leaving the parking lot.

Naomi shook her head and locked her car doors with her key fob. When she was heading inside, she noticed Red Man was no longer standing at the door.

Chapter 13
"I don't know shit"

Diamond woke up to an empty bed and an unrecognized box on her nightstand. Still half sleep, she reached for it. *What in the hell is this?* she said to herself. She rubbed both of her eyes and looked at the box again.

"U-pass, synthetic urine? Oh shit!" Diamond hollered. She forgot that she had an appointment to take her drug test. She hopped up out of the bed, not realizing how fast four days went by until now. She quickly gathered herself then shot out the door.

She got there just in time. While Diamond sat in the waiting room, she thought heavily about if the synthetic urine would work and if the officials would be able to tell the difference between the real and fake. She was terrified and still indecisive about what she was going to do. Before Diamond could figure out the answers to her questions, she was being called to the back.

"Diamond Johnson!" the lady yelled.

Diamond got up and followed her to the back.

"Verify your full name and date of birth for me."

"Diamond Larae Johnson. Date of birth is May 20, 1997."

"Thank you. This is the restroom here. No one will be in there with you, but please do not flush the toilet when you are done, or your test will be voided, and you will have to start over. This is the cup. I need urine up to here, but no more than there. Do you think you can produce enough urine, or do you need to wait?"

"I can do it."

"Great. Before I let you go inside, I need you to open your other hand and empty your pockets."

Diamond did what she was asked to do. Since she was clear, the nurse led her into the restroom. When Diamond got in there, she knew she didn't have much time to decide which urine she would use. Taking too much time would seem suspicious, so she knew she had to decide quickly. She stood in the restroom for a few seconds, with her hands on her head, trying to figure out what she was going to do.

She pulled her pants and panties down and reached up to grab the top of the U-pass bottle, then slowly slid it from the inside of her vagina. It was good she was taught how to smuggle product in her pussy or else she would have never brought the U-pass bottle in successfully.

She looked at the bottle to make sure the temperature was still accurate. Everything with the U-pass checked out. She took the top off the urine cup and started putting urine inside.

When she was finishing up, she got a knock at the restroom door. It scared her so much, the bottle of U-pass shifted back and forth in her hand, almost dropping it on the floor. Diamond's heart started pounding so hard she thought she could hear it through her chest.

"Ms. Johnson, is everything OK in there?"

Diamond focused on cleaning herself up and hiding the U-Pass without hurting herself that she never responded.

The nurse knocked on the restroom door again.

"Ms. Johnson? Is everything OK? We will open the door if we have to."

Diamond finally responded. "Everything is good."

The nurse began to get suspicious about Diamond's behavior and opened the restroom door anyways. When she went in, Diamond was on the other side of the door, about to head out. The nurse looked at Diamond, and Diamond held both of her hands up, showing nothing was there. The nurse walked past her and glanced in the toilet where only urine and tissue was inside. She looked in the small trash can and saw it was completely empty. She looked at Diamond again who watched her the entire time outside of the restroom. The nurse grabbed the urine cup out of the box and went where Diamond stood.

"May I wash my hands now?" Diamond asked.

The nurse squinted her eyes at Diamond. She knew for sure something was up, but she had no way of proving it. Diamond could tell by her facial expressions and actions that she had thoughts about what may have went on while she was in the restroom.

"Sure. Go right ahead, Ms. Johnson."

"How long before I find out the results?"

"Because this test has been ordered by a judge, you will have to wait until you go back to court."

"OK. Thank you. Am I good to leave now?"

"Do you have any more questions?" The nurse asked.

"I don't; you have answered it already. Can I leave now?"

"Yes, you may."

Diamond paced out of the office. As soon as she got back in the car, she exhaled heavily as if she was trying to release all the wind from her body. She lifted her butt up and reached inside of her pants. She pulled out the full bottle of U-pass urine and wrapped it up in a grocery bag she had lying in the car.

She put some sanitizer on her hand and wiped them with a napkin then picked up her phone to send a text message to Trill.

I got the box on the nightstand and I just finished my drug test. Thank you for getting it, but I couldn't do it. I was too scared. I couldn't do it babe. I know I failed the test, but I am woman enough to suffer the consequences and fix all of this the right way.

Trill messaged her back almost instantly.

Damn it, Diamond. That just fucked up the whole plan.

***

Trill was out working all day and all night for the past few nights. Often times, Diamond sat in the house bored, thinking about how the hell she could get money so she could finally leave Trill alone for good. That's when she came up with a good idea, but she called Naomi to see what she thought about it.

"Hey, MiMi. Are you busy?"

"Kind of. I'm at the club, about to go out and hit the stage. Why, what's up?"

"Good. I've been thinking. I need money. I can't get my job back at the club, so what do you think about me going home with a few of your drunk ass clients to make some money tonight?"

"Hell no! You ain't no fuckin' prostitute, and that shit is dangerous."

"Listen, I need this money, girl. You know I'm trying to leave this nigga alone and still be straight. I can take one of Trill's guns with me without him knowing. I'll be good. Can you help me or not?"

Naomi sucked her teeth. She didn't agree with Diamond's decision, but because she knew the reason behind it and that was her friend, she was down for whatever Diamond needed her to do.

"How can I help?"

"I'll be outside the club. Whisper to all your high end, drunk clients and tell them there is a girl that will be in the parking lot, giving them information about the after party. When they mention that, I'll know you sent them."

"I don't agree with this, Diamond."

"I'll be OK, MiMi. And if for some reason I'm not, fight to get my boys back for me and take really good care of them."

"You know I will."

"Thanks, girl. I love you."

After Diamond hung up with Naomi, she got sexy and headed over to the club. She waited in the parking lot for about an hour before people started leaving out. She saw one guy that stuck out like a sore thumb to her because he was the only one that looked lost and confused in the parking lot. She got out of her car to approach him.

"Hi, are you lost? Do you need help at all?"

The guy was so drunk, he just looked at Diamond.

She put her hand on his shoulder, looked at him and said, "It's OK. I work here. Do you need help?"

The guy responded, "Yeah. I heard something about an after party."

Diamond's face lit up. She smiled and looked at him and said, "I can help you with that. I am the after party."

Diamond opened her trench coat. She spun around, showing off her half naked body that men were always fascinated with.

The guy started smiling, and Diamond smiled back. She knew at that moment she'd captured her first victim.

"How can I sign up?" the guy asked.

"Oh, baby, it's easy. Just take me to your place, and that's when the party begins."

Without hesitation, the guy led her to his car. They didn't speak much on the way. When they arrived, she put his address in her phone. He took her to a nice home in a very quiet subdivision. She peeped out the scenery and his neighbors and got out of the car like nothing happened.

When they got inside, she looked around at how beautiful the place was. She looked for signs that he was married or if others lived in the home with him, but from what she could see, she didn't find anything.

"Make yourself at home, beautiful."

"Oh, I will," she replied.

"Would you like a beer?" he asked.

"Who the hell do you think I am? Classy women don't drink beer. Do you have some champagne or wine perhaps?"

"I don't mean to offend you. I love beer."

"Well, I don't. What about champagne or wine?"

"I have them both."

"Let me get a glass of champagne. And where's your bathroom? I want to take a shower."

"It's upstairs. You can use the one in my bedroom if you'd like. I'll be up there in a minute."

Diamond went upstairs and peeped in every door quickly and quietly. She found his bedroom and closed the door behind her then went in the bathroom and turned the shower on as if she was using it. Afterwards, Diamond left out and went back in his room to search in his drawers, hoping to find valuables. She shuffled his clothes around but didn't find anything good. When Diamond went in his nightstand drawer, there was some money, but she left it, took a few pieces of jewelry instead, and dropped it in her purse.

She heard him stumbling up the stairs and took her purse in the bathroom then closed the door. With limited time, Diamond knew she had to act fast so she could leave. The club was ending in a couple hours, and people went in and out constantly. The longer she stayed, the least amount of victims she would come across, and the less she would get out of the night.

While she stood in the bathroom, she searched around and realized he had a medicine cabinet. *Wow! This nigga health sucks, ain't it? What the hell is all of this medicine for?* she said to herself.

She searched through all of them and came across some Atarax. She poured a few in her palm and closed her fingers around it. Before he decided to come in, she left out of the bathroom with only a thong on.

"Damn, girl. You look good. I have your champagne you wanted. Come over here to me and get it."

Diamond smiled and started tiptoeing over to him in a sexy way. She stood between his legs where he sat at the edge of the bed. She turned his head a little more to her and dropped the pills in his can of beer. Feeling his hands move down toward her ass, she grabbed them stopping him.

"Oh no! None of this is free. Didn't I tell you I worked at the strip club? Where your money at, nigga?"

He reached in his pocket and pulled out a stack of money. She reached for both drinks off the nightstand and handed him his. Diamond pretended to drink some of hers then set it back where it was. She stood and watched how he guzzled his down, as she waited patiently for the meds to kick in so she could bail out on him.

"That taste weird," he mentioned to her.

Diamond shrugged her shoulders and held her hand out for the money. She started counting it, then said, "I guess this is good enough."

She pushed him back on the bed and got on top of him. She started bouncing her ass cheeks and grinding on him while he rubbed on her ass. She looked into his eyes and watched him fade away. He tried sliding Diamond's thong off, but she stopped him right then.

"Nah, fool. This ain't even that type of party. And besides, you didn't pay enough."

Right when she was done saying that, he fell into a deep sleep. She shook him many times to be sure, and he didn't budge, so she got off him and got ready to head out. Grabbing the money, she ran into the bathroom to throw on her trench coat and grab her purse. She threw the money in it, grabbed her phone out, and got an Uber en route to her. She started to head out of the room, but she turned around and grabbed her glass. She went in the kitchen to wash it out and put it in the back of the cabinet behind the others.

She put the bottom lock on the front door and ran up the street to catch her Uber which came shortly after she got outside. She got back to the club just in time for another, right before they were about to close for the night. After being in the parking lot again, she walked up to a fine guy and asked him where he was getting ready to go. He told her he was headed to his house, and she offered to join him. He agreed to it and she got in his car. He didn't seem as drunk as the last guy, but he had a nice car and was hoping she could get just as much money out of him as she did the first.

He made small conversation with her while he drove.

"I feel like I know you, what's your name?"

Diamond looked at him and said, "No, you don't know me."

"Do you work at the club?"

"Yeah, I do," she lied.

"Yeah, I thought so. So, what are we gonna do at my place tonight?"

"It all depends on how much you are trying to spend."

He pulled the car over, and Diamond began to get nervous.

He reached in his pocket, and Diamond slowly placed her hand inside of her purse on the gun she stole from Trill. The guy pulled out some money and held it in Diamond's face.

"How much is it?" she asked.

"I don't know; you can count it. I've been wanting a private dance from you for a long time now, Dream, or should I call you Diamond now that we aren't at the club?"

Diamond raised her eyebrows and started to get out the car, but he stopped her. She knew for sure that he was one of Trill's guys, and no way in hell she wanted this to get back to him. She felt like it was a set up, and she wanted out.

"Get off of me! Who the fuck are you? You work for Trill, don't you?"

The more she stared in his face, the more he looked familiar to her.

"No, I don't work for Trill, but my job requires me to find out everything about him, everyone he's around, and the operation he has."

"Are you the fuckin' feds, brah?"

"No, not really." He pulled out his badge and said, "I work for Charleston County Police Department."

"Oh, hell no! I'm out," Diamond told him. She tried getting out the car again, but he stopped her once more.

"I'm not a prostitute, just to let you know. I'm a stripper, and there's a huge difference."

He started to laugh. "I know you aren't. I know quite a bit about you, actually. I also know that the man you are with is very dangerous and controlling."

"Listen, I don't know shit about him and what he has going on. It ain't any of my business, and if I did know, I wasn't snitching anyways," she told him.

"Well, if you decide to change your mind, here's my card. If you help me, I can help you. I know what happened to your brother. I know that the case is still unsolved, and it's been put aside. What I can say is, if you can help me with what I need to know about Trill and his drug organization, I can get that case opened again. We both know you know more than what you are telling me."

"Do you know what will happen to me if I snitch on him? Him or his peoples would fuckin' kill me! I have kids. I'm not trying to get caught up in any of his shit."

"You're already dealing with him, darling. I'm afraid it's too late. You're already involved. Witness protection is always an option."

Diamond snatched the business card out of his hands and got out of the car.

"Do you want me to take you back to the club?"

"No thanks. I'll walk!"

"Don't forget about what I told you, Diamond. We could really use each other's help!" the officer hollered.

Chapter 14

"Snitches get Stitches"

Diamond knew she failed the drug test because she decided to be honest and used her own. So when she heard the news in the courtroom, it was no surprise to her. With a clean drug test, she would be one step closer to bringing her boys home, but now, there were steps that needed to be taken to make things right. She was willing to take each step without leaping over any, to be able to see their little faces and hold them in her arms again.

Now that they knew she had done drugs previously, the judge ordered her rehabilitation. It was a must that she was clean from drugs before she came back for another court date two months later. She was also forced to take parenting classes that she thought was irrelevant. She knew who the problem was; it wasn't her, but since she decided not to be honest, it left her no choice but to deal with all that she was being put through.

Diamond called Naomi and told her what happened and what was next to come. As usual, Naomi pushed her to do what was right and promised to be by her side every step of the way. Naomi was definitely a real friend to Diamond, one that many would die to have and one you should never let go once you came across them.

"I want you to remember what I told you. I'm ready to make the big move when you are. The offer will always be on the table. Whatever

I can do to help you get away from this idiot and get the boys back, just know I'm gonna do it. I'm only one call away," Naomi told her.

While Diamond sat in the car talking to Naomi, the sun beamed in her eyes. When she pulled down her sun visor, the cop's card fell on her lap. Diamond sat on the phone quietly, thinking about if she should use the card or not.

"Did you hear me, girl? Are you still there?" Naomi asked.

"Yeah, my bad. I'm still here. I heard everything you said, and I appreciate you for all your help, but I think I know what I'm going to do to fix all of this."

"Well, what is it? Tell me," Naomi begged.

"I'd rather not right now. I'll let you know when I'm more comfortable doing so. I don't think it's safe to say yet."

After Diamond got off the phone with Naomi, she was headed to get something to eat. She hadn't put anything on her stomach all day, and it was beginning to ache from starvation. With everything going on, she didn't have an appetite, but she knew she had to eat, so she was going to force it down.

She went to a Chinese restaurant and got some takeout. She sat inside and waited for her food to be ready. While she was waiting, she took the card out of her pocket and stared at it. She replayed everything that happened in the car with the cop that night. Hearing the things he told her made her wonder if she should turn on Trill while she had the chance. The more she looked at the card, the more she began to believe that maybe he was the help that she'd been looking for all along.

She made the call but forgot to block her number.

"Hello, this is Officer Burrell."

"Hi, this is Diamond."

"Oh, Diamond." He responded, but she could hear his voice getting lower when he said that.

"It's so good to finally hear from you," he said.

"Yeah, I guess. Um, I thought about what you said the other night. Is there any chance that we could meet?"

"Uh, yeah, sure, sure thing. How about uh, at the parking lot of a restaurant?"

"No! Are you crazy? I can't risk being seen with you. That's not private enough. What about we meet near those abandon buildings on Andrews Boulevard?"

"Yeah, uh, sure. Whatever works for you. I appreciate you reaching out. I'll be there in half an hour. See you soon."

As soon as Diamond hung up the phone, someone in the restaurant tapped her on the shoulder. She jumped frantically and turned around slowly.

"Ma'am, your order is ready," the guy told her.

Diamond held her chest and exhaled. She smiled and told the guy thank you before quickly getting up to grab her food and then heading out the door to meet Officer Burrell.

When she pulled up to the meeting spot, she saw a black Tahoe parked. The windows were darkly tinted, and she couldn't tell who sat behind the steering wheel or if anyone else was inside. She was anxious, so instead of driving any closer, she called to confirm that it was him.

"It's me in the Tahoe. Pull up closer beside me, and hop in," he said to her as soon as he answered.

Diamond was afraid, not knowing if it was a setup or not. She drove up slowly and constantly checked her surroundings. Something didn't seem right to her. It felt strange, but she knew it was something she had to do. Nobody knew where she was and who she was meeting, so if anything went left, she would be on her own. Unfortunately, she didn't have Trill's gun this time.

She got out of her car and walked up to the passenger side of the truck slowly, peeping inside the windows while she approached. When she got close enough, the passenger door swung open.

"It's cool. Hop in," she heard Officer Burrell say.

She got in the car, still uneasy about all of it.

"Thank you so much for reaching out to me."

"Yeah, not a problem," Diamond said while she looked around.

"How do I know if you aren't wearing a wire or recording me? Why do we have to be in your car? Why can't we go in mine?" Diamond asked.

Officer Burrell pulled up his shirt, showing off his perfectly laid six pack to prove to Diamond he wasn't wired.

"And what about the recorder?" she asked.

He opened his phone and showed her no apps were opened or recording her then set it on the dashboard.

"I'm being completely honest with you, as I expect for you to be with me. If it makes you happier, feel free to search whatever."

Diamond didn't pass up the opportunity. She opened the glove box, shuffled around in the back seat, checked the storage on the doors, lifted up the floor mats, and checked inside of the arm rest, and she did not find anything else.

Diamond leaned her back on the door and crossed her arms.

"OK. I guess you're good."

"You have to trust me, sweetie."

"You're a fuckin' cop. I don't know how much you expect me to trust you when I don't know your ass."

"I get it, but if that's the case, why did you ask me to meet?"

"For many reasons. First, I need to know how you knew who I was."

"Well, I saw you when your brother got shot. I was one of the officers that responded to the call. Besides that, I only knew you from the club. I had my eyes on you for a while there and then you disappeared on me, until I saw you when I did a traffic stop on your dude. Now that you are dealing with Trill, you've been on the radar and have more eyes on you than you may realize."

"Wait, that was you?"

"Yeah, you both were acting strange that night. What was that about?"

"Right before you stopped us, we had a little argument, nothing major. Don't worry about it," Diamond lied. "So listen, I asked you to meet me because I thought about what we talked about the other night. I am willing to help you with Trill and everything he has going on if you can help me."

"I told you I can get your brother's case opened back up. That's not a problem."

"I know you have said that, but there's another issue. If you can help me with this, I'm in a hundred percent."

Officer Burrell's eyebrows rose, and a sign of suspense showed on his face.

"I have a big problem. Recently, my kids were taken from me. It wasn't my fault why all of this happened, but I'm scared to tell the truth."

"You would have to tell me the truth so I can help you."

"One day, Trill and I got into a physical fight, and my twin boys heard us and came running in the room to get him off of me. Trill's adrenaline was pumping, and he knocked one of my boys in the face. They went to school the next week, and the teacher saw the knot on his head. My kids told them what happened, and now they don't feel like they are safe at home. CPS is involved now. There was a court ordered drug test that I took, and I failed, only because Trill made me snort cocaine and smoke weed with him.

"I never did drugs before I got with Trill. He always forced me to do it with him. The night you stopped us was my first time sniffing cocaine, and I passed out. That's why I was acting weird at the traffic stop." Diamond continued.

"Well, I definitely wasn't expecting anything like this."

"Can you help or not?"

"I think I can."

"No, I need to know for sure, because if you can't help me get my kids back and find out who killed my brother, I'm not saying shit."

"You might want to think twice about that. You need to let me help you while I can. The more time that passes, the deeper this shit gets, and at some point, this offer will no longer be available. Your boy is wanted by every fuckin' body. CCPD and the streets, but I'm sure you know that already."

"Well I'm willing to talk as long as my name stays clear. Help with my brother's case as much as you can and get my babies home for sure. One last question, if I do this, how do I know that you will hold up your end of the deal?"

"What reason do I have not to?"

Diamond's phone buzzed from a text message she received.

"Hold on a second, he just sent me a message... He said meet him at the money spot tonight at eight p.m."

"What's the money spot?"

"The trap house, silly."

"Where is that?" Officer Burrell asked.

"Not so fast. I'll go to the trap alone, and I'll tell you what happens. I'm going to reach out to you. Don't reach out to me or the deal's off, and I'll figure this shit out on my own."

"I got it. I'll wait to hear from you." He agreed.

Diamond got out of the truck and went back to her car where she responded to Trill's text before pulling off. Diamond and Officer Burrell went their separate ways. While trying to past time, Diamond stopped by Ms. Mable's place.

Diamond knew it was a while since she last went by, but as soon as she saw Ms. Mable, she noticed how different she looked. She was much thinner than the last time Diamond saw her. They hugged each other, and Diamond held her tightly.

"Have you been taking care of yourself?" Diamond asked.

"I've been doing the best that I can. I can't be selfish; the community needs me."

"Ms. Mable, I understand because I have been one of many that needed your help too, but you have to take care of yourself. Are you eating at all? You have lost a lot of weight. How much did you lose?"

"Well I'm sick, baby. It's to be expected. My time is winding down. I don't know how much longer I'm going to be here to be honest with you. This lupus is taking a toll on me."

Diamond held her, not wanting to let her go for any reason at all. Ms. Mable started coughing badly. Diamond turned her loose and checked to make sure she was OK. She saw how weak she had become and how much her hands shook.

"Sit here. I'll go get you a glass of water. With all that coughing, your throat will be as dry as a desert," Diamond joked.

Ms. Mable tried laughing, but Diamond saw how difficult it was for her to use her facial muscles.

"Sit tight and don't move. I'll be right back."

Ms. Mable continued to cough and nodded her head up and down. When Diamond came back with the glass of water, she handed it to her, but she could hardly hold it tight enough; she almost spilled it all over herself.

"Enough about me. How have y'all been? Where are my boys?" Ms. Mable asked.

"Well, we are doing OK. The boys are fine. They keep me busy. I don't know if you remember my friend Naomi, but they are over at her place," Diamond lied.

She looked at her phone and realized that she needed to get to Trill's meeting soon.

"Ms. Mable, I have to get going now, but I promise I will be back for you. Not to see you, but to get you. I'm getting somethings in order, and soon, I'll be able to bring you to my place and take care of you."

"Oh no, baby. I've been doing this a long time. I can handle myself."

"I'm not accepting no for an answer. You have done so much for everyone else, it's about time somebody takes care of you. In a couple months, I'll be back to get you."

"OK, baby. I'll be right here waiting on you. I need to see my boys before then."

"I'll bring them back soon."

They both stood up and hugged one last time.

While Diamond made her way to her destination, she thought about Ms. Mable and how crucial it was for everything to fall back in place soon. She was depending on Officer Burrell to help her out of all this shit she somehow got herself into. The more time that passed, the more she hated being around Trill and realized how much she couldn't wait to end things with him. She was over it all; getting physically abused, living on a budget, depending on a man, being controlled, and doing things she never wanted to do.

Although she didn't have much before him, she wanted her old life back. She'd realize, her desire for money and materialistic things wasn't worth the shit she went through to get it. She wanted to get it the right way and be happy. Instead, she had everything she wanted along with unhappiness and a regretful life she was now living.

When Diamond got to the spot, she dreaded on going inside. Once she finally went inside, she saw that Trill seemed really upset. He didn't acknowledge Diamond with a hug and a kiss like he normally did. She thought, *well maybe he knows what I did behind his back,* but she kept it cool until he mentioned it to her himself. She was so paranoid; she didn't know what to think or believe anymore. She thought he was only upset with her, but then he started cussing and flipping out on everyone.

"I don't know what you motherfuckers are doing out here in these streets, but keep y'all fuckin' mouth shut. Too many people are coming to me about them being watched by who they believe are undercover cops. Just remember, if your fuck up jeopardizes my business in any way, I will fuckin' kill you. Do I make myself clear?"

Everyone agreed with Trill, and as soon as everyone began to part ways, Diamond saw Black walk in. She hadn't seen that nigga in over three years, but she wondered what the fuck he was doing there in Trill's place.

Chapter 15

"Don't get caught"

After Diamond's class, she took out her phone to call Naomi to tell her all that she'd been doing behind Trill's back and put her on point about the cop. When she looked at her phone, she realized that she had a voicemail from an unsaved number which turned out to be Officer Burrell's. She was a little irked to see that he called her when she told him not to.

She listened to the voicemail to see what it was he couldn't wait to tell her, but the message didn't say much. All he said was, "Diamond, call me ASAP. We need to meet. I have some valuable information about your brother that I think you would want to hear," and she called him back immediately.

"Hey, Officer Burrell, it's Diamond. I got your message. What was it you wanted to talk to me about?"

"Diamond, I don't know if you will be happy about what I have to tell you, but I would rather meet up and tell you in person."

"I am leaving my court ordered parenting classes. It's not too far from where we met the first time. I can meet you at the same spot. I'll be there in five minutes."

"I am just around the corner; I should be arriving when you are."

Diamond arrived before he did. She constantly looked around to make sure no one was watching or following her. She knew how much danger she was putting herself in, going behind Trill's back and working with this cop, but she needed his help for sure.

Officer Burrell was taking too long, and she started to feel leery of his actions. She picked up the phone to call and see what the holdup was, but as soon as she did, he pulled in. She was already outside of her car before he made a complete stop. She hopped in and was dying to hear the news that he had for her.

"This must be important since you called me."

"Well Diamond, I think it really is. Brace yourself for what I am about to tell you because this isn't good."

Diamond's eyes began to water as her mind started to wander.

"What is it? Tell me," Diamond said.

"Well, Diamond, after going through everything in your brother's case—"

Diamond cut him short.

"Let me guess, you didn't find anything and there's nothing you can do. I fuckin' knew it. This was all a waste of time."

She got out of the car and started heading back to hers. Officer Burrell rolled down the passenger window and hollered to her.

"I can see that you have had a bad experience with police in the past. Like I've told you before, if we are going to be in this together, you will have to give me the benefit of the doubt and put some kind of trust in me. You will have to believe that I am here to help you just as much as you are here to help me. We are working together. You were completely wrong about everything you just said. Now do me a favor and get back inside so I can tell you what's going on. Let me talk and tell you why I asked you to meet me here. I'm sure you don't want everyone in our business."

Diamond walked up to his window, embarrassed about what she said and the way she acted. "I was wrong?"

"Yes, you were," Officer Burrell said.

Diamond got back in with her ears opened and her mouth shut.

"I'm listening," she told him.

"Like I was saying, I went through your brother's files and found some valuable information. There are many reasons why the police department wants Trill in their custody. One being because of the organization that he is running, and the second is because he is a person of interest in your brother's case."

"What?" Diamond was shocked. "Wait, wait, wait, wait a minute. So you are telling me that he killed my brother? No, there must be some mistake. Ain't no way."

"No, Diamond, we are not saying that he killed your brother, but quite a few people believe that he had something to do with it, or someone in his circle did. If he did not kill your brother, we believe that he knows who did do it."

Diamond sat in the passenger seat quietly, trying to take in all the information that was just given to her. She started thinking. She started thinking a lot about Trill's actions and the things that he said.

"The other day when I met him at the trap house, I did notice something very suspicious that I have never noticed before."

"What was it, Diamond? That may be the big break we have been looking for."

"I noticed one of my brother's old friends walk inside. I hadn't seen him since my brother died. They were really close friends, but he disappeared after we buried Rod. It was always strange to me that he never tried reaching out."

"What was his friend's name?"

"He goes by Black."

"Oh yeah, we know Black. We have had many run-ins with him before."

"I think he was a bad influence on my brother. I believe that's why he's dead because of the company he kept. He wasn't a bad guy. He was not a street nigga at all. My mother wasn't shit and didn't care about us. That caused Rod to make poor decisions because he wanted to make sure we had what we needed. I will not sit here and say that what he did was right, but thanks to him, neither of us went to foster care. He was trying to help me with my twin boys and take care of the both of us, but I wish he would have listened to me and that our last conversation wasn't an argument. We had a fucked-up childhood. All he wanted was to make it better; instead, it became worse. I miss him. They took something special from me I can never get back." Diamond cried.

"It's OK, Diamond. It's OK. You are a young, smart girl. I can tell that you are on a path to providing a better life for you and your kids just from you sitting right here next to me. Not many people have the courage to do this, but look at you. No, we can't bring Rod back, but we can eliminate something like that from happening to you or any of your kids. I will do all that I can to get your boys back home with you, to make sure that y'all are safe from all of this, and to find out who is responsible for the hurt that was caused to you from losing a brother. We are making progress. I found out quite a bit since meeting you three days ago."

"Thank you, Officer Burrell. Let me know if there is anything else that you find out, and I will reach out to you for the same reason. I think I should get going now. Oh, and by the way, I have more trust in you than I have in any other man."

Diamond was even more stressed now. She couldn't shake the thought of Trill killing her brother or him knowing all along who did without ever mentioning it to her. She knew he had a cold heart and didn't give a fuck about too many, but she really believed that out of all people, he would not do her like everybody else.

***

Trill wasn't at the house too often these days. He said he was out making money now that they had more expenses to keep up with, but it was always in the back of her mind that he was over at Treasure's place. If he was, it wasn't much she could say or do anyways. She knew the consequences that would come behind it. She often found herself going along with whatever it was he was doing to protect herself from being abused. Having him gone most of the time didn't bother her much for that reason. It was much safer for her that way.

Now that she was talking to the cop, she knew it would only be a matter of time before someone saw her or found out. Trill always left a gun at the house, so she went to get it so it would be close to her. That was her only way of protecting herself if something were to happen. That same night, she searched the house for it everywhere.

She knew she placed it underneath the mattress after the night she had it. That's where they kept it, but for some odd reason, it wasn't there. She knew a gun was somewhere near, even if it wasn't the one she previously snuck. She started searching everywhere in the room. She searched the kids' room, the bathrooms, and even the hall closets, only to come up empty handed.

She went downstairs where he left some of his bags and shoe boxes and began to search it, but she stopped. He had so much clothes and boxes to go through, so she figured she'd take the easier route first and start searching the kitchen and living room. Still, no gun was found. She went back to the closet where his belongings were. That was the last place in the house it could be. She knew how time consuming it was and prepared herself. While she was looking through his boxes, she came across some weed and some coke.

Diamond pulled it out of the boxes and pushed everything she had on her lap on the floor beside her. She smelled the bag of weed and closed her eyes slowly, taking in the musky scent of the compressed leaves Trill called loud. She was tempted to smoke it. She thought about how at ease the high would make her, but it would only push her back in the process she'd already made much progress in. Diamond snapped swiftly and threw the drugs back in the box. *I can't do this shit!* she said to herself.

She continued looking through the bags of clothes. She had one of his pants in her hand, and when she lifted it to toss it to the side with all the others, she felt something in the pocket. She dug inside and pulled out a bracelet.

She held it in her hands and started weeping, covering her mouth with one of her hands. The hand that held the bracelet started shaking uncontrollably.

"Noooooo! Why!" Diamond started yelling.

She started to pick up her phone to call Naomi but then she realized she heard a car out front. Diamond lifted her head to see if the car was in her driveway, and it was. It was Trill. She put the bracelet back in the pants pocket where she found it, threw the clothes back in the bag, and placed the shoe boxes back how they were as quickly as she could.

She snatched her phone off the floor and ran upstairs then hopped in the bed and turned the TV on. She dried her tears with the blanket on the bed. Squealing could be heard from front door followed by heavy footsteps hitting the hardwood floors before the sound of Trill's voice.

"Baby, are you still wake?"

Diamond heard him coming up the stairs and tried fronting as if nothing happened. As soon as he approached the room, Diamond responded.

"Hey, babe. How was your night?"

Chapter 16

"The walls are closing in"

Diamond could not wait for Trill to leave the next morning so she could make some phone calls. All night long, she thought about the bracelet she found in his pocket. She was starting to believe what Officer Burrell told her, not that it ever escaped her mind completely.

While she lay in bed, she thought deeper about things, like how Trill ended up with the bracelet her brother stole before he died. She thought about why he targeted her at the club and how long he and Black knew each other. She even thought about Naomi working with Trill after feeling like Naomi pressured her into dealing with him.

Besides Ms. Mable, Naomi was the only other person she could turn to that was capable of helping her. She felt bad about telling Naomi everything that happened because, now, she wasn't sure if she could be trusted. At this point, Diamond didn't know who was on her side.

Diamond waited and waited for Trill to leave. She started getting impatient and began doing things around the house to past time. She didn't say much to him, but she knew that had to change pronto. She didn't want to tip him off about anything she knew. As hard as it was for her, she had to pretend nothing ever happened.

When she walked downstairs, she saw Trill in the closet where she found the bracelet. Diamond gasped and stopped on the stairs, not realizing how obvious she made it seem that something was wrong. When she put everything back in the closet, it wasn't like he had it before because she was rushing. If he noticed, her cover would be blown.

He acknowledged her and asked her if she was OK.

"Yeah, I just realized I forgot to do something upstairs."

Diamond turned around and ran back upstairs, went into her bathroom, and closed the door behind her. She threw her elbows on the countertop and leaned over in the mirror. She tried easing her breathing to calm herself down. *Shit! That was close. I gotta get out of here. When is this nigga leaving?* she asked herself.

Calm down, Diamond. Calm down. You got this. Act normal, she said again.

Right after she said that, she walked out of the bathroom, looking at herself in the mirror, and when she faced forward, Trill was standing in front of her.

"Shit! You scared me!" she told him.

"Yeah, I bet! What the fuck has been up with you lately?"

"What do you mean?" Diamond asked.

"Give me your phone!" Trill demanded.

Diamond handed over her phone to him. He searched through the call logs and only found his number along with business numbers. He went to her text messages and only found texts from him. He went to her voicemail, and it was empty.

"Nothing is going on with me. I haven't been myself since the boys left, that's all," she told him.

Trill looked at Diamond with a scowling look then handed her back her phone.

"Give me a hug and a kiss. I'm leaving. Treasure needs me to get Nevaeh today."

Diamond rolled her eyes as she gave him a hug. After finding out the truth about him and Treasure, she didn't trust him around her. It didn't bother her as much as it did in the beginning, because the feelings she had for him were slowly fading away after all the hell he'd caused her.

"That's exciting! What are y'all gonna do together?" Diamond asked him, pretending to show interest in his plans.

"We will go shopping, out to eat, and do girly stuff. I guess I'll take her to get her nails painted. I don't know."

"That sounds like a fun day. I wish I could come. It would be a great time for me to meet her," Diamond lied.

"Give me kiss. I need to get going," Trill said, ignoring the comment Diamond made that she wasn't being honest about anyways.

Trill headed downstairs, and Diamond followed. She stood in the door and watched him get in his car. She closed and locked the door but went to sit by the window until he finally left. As soon as she saw him leave, she called Naomi.

"Hey, girl," Naomi answered.

"Don't hey girl me!" Diamond said intensely.

"What's wrong, Diamond?"

"Are you workin' with Trill?"

"Hell no! Now what made you think some shit like that?"

"I think this nigga killed my brother, and you pressured me into talking to him at the club. Was this some sort of setup, MiMi? Just tell me the truth!"

"No, Diamond! I only knew of him. I'm not workin' with that nigga! You are trippin' for real!

Tell me this, if I was working with him, why would he tell you to stay away from me? Wouldn't he want me to be around you to keep tabs on you? And another thing, he would know everything that you're doing behind his back right now if I was. So, tell me, you think he killed Rod?"

Diamond realized Naomi made a valid point. She felt awful about how she went off on her.

"Yeah. I think he killed Rod. I found the bracelet in his pocket that Rod stole right before he got shot. After he stole it, I wore it out after he told me not to. After he died, I was over at Ms. Mable's, and someone went into our place and took almost everything that him and his boys got from the lick. One of those things were the bracelet."

"Oh my gosh! How do you know it's the same bracelet?"

"I know it is! Let me tell you how, because it had a deep scrape on the side, and I know. I know that it is."

"Well, what are you gonna do now?"

"Well I've been working with this cop. He wants to arrest Trill and seize his organization, and I want justice for Rod and to get my kids back. We made a deal, exchange for exchange. I'm going to call him with more information and see what he has for me."

"Please be careful, Diamond! Call me back and tell me as soon as you're done."

"OK. I will."

Diamond called Officer Burrell and told him what she found and everything about it.

"Is there any way you can get that bracelet and give it to me so we can get some prints off of it?"

Diamond looked outside to make sure Trill didn't come back, then looked in the direction of the closet where it was.

"Yeah. I can do that."

"Great. Text me once you get it. We can hit the meeting spot afterwards. Don't forget. I need to get going though. I'm finding out more information on your brother's case."

Diamond hung up with him and went digging in the bag again to get the bracelet. She saw the jeans that she remembered it was in, but when she went inside of the pockets, they were emptied. She checked all the shoe boxes to see if the coke and weed was still there, but it was gone.

She went back in the bag and checked each of his pants pockets then threw them in a pile to the side. She was down to the last pair of pants, but still no bracelet.

"Shit!" she yelled.

Where the hell is that bracelet? Please don't tell me he took the bracelet.

There were only shirts left in the bag, but she kept looking. She shook each shirt and threw it in a pile next to the pants. She pulled out the very last shirt and saw the shiny bracelet lying at the bottom of the black garbage bag. Diamond grabbed the bracelet and slid it in her back pocket.

"Yeeeeess! Thank God!" she hollered.

Diamond grabbed her phone and sent a text to Officer Burrell.

I have it. Be there in 15 minutes, the text read.

Great. See you then, he responded.

Diamond threw on a shirt, jeans, and some sneakers. She didn't waste any time heading out the door. She was running a little behind time, so she sped to the meeting spot. She was so focused on getting to Officer Burrell in time, that she didn't check her surroundings like she normally did. Something told her they should meet someplace different, but she ignored her intuition.

When she arrived, he was already there, so she hopped in his car. She handed him over the bracelet, but instead of him touching it, he had her drop it into an evidence bag.

"My prints are on these. What does that mean for me?" Diamond asked.

"I have you covered. No worries," he told her. "I have more information for you if you'd like to hear it."

"Hell yeah! Tell me more!"

"We believe that Red Man is Black's brother, and Red Man is an accomplice in this case. The three folks we are looking at are Red Man, Trill, and Black. We believe they all were working together to have Rod killed."

"How is that possible? Black told Rod about the lick that night. They were like brothers, why would Black be involved in any of this? Are you sure about this?"

"Most of these murders are done by someone close to the victims, especially when they are so young and innocent like Rod was. You asked why Black would want Rod dead. They were close, but why not? Because of that reason, nobody would suspect that he would do it, right?"

"I never knew Black had a brother," Diamond said.

"That's how it's supposed to be. Just like you didn't know Black and Trill knew each other. Criminals keep a lot of secrets."

"So did Red Man know who I was the entire time I was working at his club?"

"I'm not quite sure, to be honest, but maybe."

"Damn! Why would I be a target though? After all these years, why bother me?"

"They weren't. The city is so small, you fell right in, all by yourself. Maybe they feel like you owe them something. Maybe your brother held on to something that belongs to them and they are trying to get it back from you."

"Rod didn't have anything. They took all that he had, like that bracelet."

"I'm still working on this. What I want you to do is hang with him more at the trap house and visit the club more. I need you to find out information we don't already know. We are getting closer to moving in on them. In just a matter of time, we will have them in custody."

"That sounds good and all, but you haven't mentioned my kids much," Diamond pointed out.

"I have a friend who works for child protective services who is putting something together for us. Your kids are safe. She mentioned to me that they ask about you a lot and want to come back home. All of this takes time, Diamond."

"Can you have her tell my babies that I love them, and that I can't wait to see them again?"

"Sure, I can do that!"

"OK. So what's the plan to capture these motherfuckers?" Diamond asked.

"I'll text you later to call me. I will tell you what the plan is then. I still need to gather more information, so when we get them, we can keep them in custody. Get close to him. Whatever you can find out will help tremendously."

"I can do that. I'll stay by my phone."

"If you need to call me before I reach out to you, then call me," Officer Burrell said.

Diamond went back to her car, and Officer Burrell pulled off first. When Diamond left, she looked in the rearview mirror and realized the car that was behind her had been following her for a few miles. She began to worry about who it was. She turned her head to look back, but she didn't see the car anymore. She kept driving then looked to the left and saw the car that was behind her, speed off past her.

It wasn't Trill's car for sure, but she wondered how long the anonymous person had been following or even watching her. She wondered if they knew the car she was in belonged to a cop. The streets didn't play about snitches. If anything got back to Trill, she knew she would be dead, literally.

Diamond called Naomi. She told her that she met with the cop to give him the bracelet and she found out some more information in the process. Diamond told her she needed her to meet her at her place because of how scared she was to be there alone. She promised to explain everything to her then, and Naomi agreed to meet her.

Diamond rushed home and started packing while she waited on Naomi to arrive. She waited around for the text from Officer Burrell, but it still hadn't come through. The weird activity with the anonymous person watching her freaked her out. She knew she wouldn't be able to hold her composure around Trill much longer, now that she was finding out more about him. He would soon realize that she knew more than he thought she did. She knew it wasn't safe for her to stay at home, so when Naomi came, she would leave her car home and have Naomi take her to Ms. Mable's place.

While Diamond packed, she saw the gun that she was looking for, sitting up behind her purses on the closet shelf. She was upstairs in complete silence when she heard the front door opened. She mimicked what she saw Trill do with his guns and tucked it in the back of her pants. She pulled her shirt down to cover the handle then grabbed her packed bag to take downstairs since Naomi was finally there. When she walked downstairs, she slowed her pace when she saw Trill standing with his back against the closed door, and he did not look happy.

Chapter 17

"When it Ends"

Diamond dropped her bags on the stairs where she remained. Trill walked toward her, but she didn't move. Diamond was at her breaking point, and for the first time, she stood up for herself that night, not allowing him to break her down any longer.

"So, who was that you met today?"

"Who was that following me?" she asked.

"Answer my got damn question!" Trill yelled. "Is there someone else, Diamond? How long have you been seeing him?"

"That was the twins' dad. I found him and told him I needed his help because of what happened to them," Diamond lied.

Trill breathed heavily in her face with his eyebrows wrinkled and lips sealed tightly together. Diamond stood tall in front of him. He wrapped his hand around her jaw and squeezed tightly. His veins started popping out of his hands, and Diamond couldn't say a word.

She used both of her hands, trying to loosen his on her face, but Trill was one strong son of a bitch. It didn't help her much.

"Don't fuckin' lie to me!" He hollered louder. She felt specks of saliva hitting her face in the process.

Diamond started crying since she realized Trill wasn't turning her loose anytime soon and he was hurting her. She tried mumbling, and she kept trying to take his hands off of her. He loosened his hand a little. It was enough for Diamond to wiggle her jaws to ease the pain. He finally let her go completely and walked off from her.

"So where were you going with your bags? Were you gonna run off and leave me without saying goodbye, after all I've done for you? You are an ungrateful bitch!" he said as he looked around.

Diamond didn't say a word. She eased closer to the door, slowly but surely. Trill walked around the house and hollered more and more. He was seemingly angry, and Diamond already knew what type of night it would be for her. She found herself wishing she was alone that night as she was for the past few weeks.

Trill walked to the closet where all his clothes and shoes were.

"Were you in this closet?" he asked.

"Yeah!"

"Why the hell were you in here?"

"I was looking for something," Diamond explained.

"Did you find what you were looking for?"

"No, but I found something I wasn't expecting to see. Trill, do you know my brother Rod?" Diamond continued.

"Yeah, I know of that motherfucker."

"Why did you not tell me this?"

"What happened to him had nothing to do with you," Trill said.

"Did you kill him?"

"Why the fuck are you asking me about that punk ass nigga?"

"Because he's my fuckin' brother who didn't deserve to die. I found a bracelet in your pants pocket that Rod had before he got shot. So, tell me, how did you get it?"

"It doesn't matter. How he got it was the problem."

Diamond's phone buzzed from a text notification and with Trill standing near her, she knew it was either two other people. Trill heard her phone and charged at her.

"Where is it? Give it to me!" he hollered.

"No! I'm not giving it to you!" Diamond hollered back.

As they tussled for her phone, Naomi arrived. She saw Diamond and Trill's car in the driveway, so she parked a few doors down and ran across the neighbors' lawn, so Trill had no chance of seeing her. When she got closer to the house, she heard loud arguing. She peeped through one of the windows and saw Diamond on the floor with Trill on top of her. Naomi rushed through the front door. Diamond and Trill paused to look at her. Trill was confused about her being there, but Diamond was relieved that she had finally came.

"You better get the fuck off of her right now, damnit!" Naomi hollered.

Trill got up slowly from Diamond and walked toward Naomi. Naomi ran over and grabbed Trill's gun that slid across the floor when he tussled with Diamond.

"Or what?" Trill asked.

Naomi pointed the gun at Trill as Diamond got up off the floor.

"No, MiMi, no! Don't shoot him!" Diamond yelled.

"Better listen to your friend," Trill told Naomi.

Diamond hollered to Trill, "Tell me! How did you know Rod, and who shot him? How did you get that bracelet he had?"

Trill stopped and turned around toward Diamond. Naomi withdrew the gun but kept it in her hand in case she needed it later.

"Your fuckin' brother and his boys robbed the wrong motherfuckers. They hit up Treasure's house, put a gun up in her face in front of my daughter, and stole our shit. That bracelet you found was Treasure's. I bought it for her when we first started talking. Nobody steals from me and get away with it! That motherfucker had to die," Trill admitted.

"Why was Rod the only one to get shot? Black was with him, along with others. I saw Black at the trap that night you called the meeting. You have him in your corner, but he's double crossing you. He was the one who told them about the lick. Why didn't that motherfucker die long time ago?"

"Oh yeah? So he told them about it, huh? I'm gonna deal with that nigga! He lied. He told me he heard on the streets who robbed her place and took our shit. He shot Rod then went to get our shit back so he could prove that he was about that shit because he wanted to roll with me. He offered to shoot your brother. I never told him to. So this nigga playing both sides?"

"Black killed my brother, and you knew this entire time?"

Trill did a thin lip grin and walked closer to Diamond.

"Listen, baby girl…"

Diamond pulled the gun from her pants and held it with both hands pointing it at Trill.

"So you're taking after your brother and stealing from me too? Put my gun down."

"Nigga, fuck you! I am so sick and tired of being your ragdoll. I have lost everything because of you. Ever since I got with you, my life has been in shambles, and I have lived every single day unhappily. You lied to me from day one, and you caused my kids to be taken away from me, the only people I had left after Rod. You forced me to do drugs, you have me on the radar with the cops, you turned me into a criminal, and I'm not living another fuckin' day with you! After I pull this trigger, Black will be next on the list to fuckin' die." Diamond cried.

"You don't know shit about a gun. Look at you. Your hands are shaking like your ass did on the stage at the strip club," Trill joked.

He walked toward Diamond more, and she eased the trigger back slowly.

"You aren't gonna shoot me! You need me!" He bragged.

"But I don't," Naomi said.

Right after she said that, a bright light flashed before their eyes and their ears rang terribly. Blood splattered on the couch that Trill stood near, and he dropped to the floor. Diamond ran over to Naomi, hugging and thanking her. She knew she didn't have the guts to do it herself. Even if she did, she probably would have missed anyways.

"Watch out. Let me make sure this motherfucker is dead," Naomi said.

She walked over to Trill and stood over him, watching how the blood pooled out of his mouth and how much he suffered to survive. Diamond walked over to them and looked down at him on the floor. She wiped her tears and said her last words to him. "It's over for you, bitch! Now tell me, how does it feel knowing many that depend on you will hurt like me and the twins did?"

"You… you bitch!" Trill struggled to say.

"I'm no longer your bitch. Rot in hell, motherfucker! That was for me, the twins, and Rod!"

Right after Diamond said that, Trill became lifeless.

"What do we do now, MiMi?" Diamond panicked.

"Let's get the fuck out of here," Naomi replied.

"Wait a minute. I have a better idea. There's someone that may be able to help us."

Diamond grabbed her phone and saw Officer Burrell sent her the text earlier. He was just the person she needed to talk to.

"Who are you calling?" Naomi asked.

"Remember that cop I told you I was meeting?"

"Why? Why the hell are you calling a cop? Don't you know he will have to call this shit in? We can't go to jail for murder."

"We have to call someone. I'd rather call him than anyone else. He will be able to help us. I'll tell him what happened. That's the only way he will be able to help. We can't run away. Imagine how that would look."

Diamond called him, but he didn't answer. She paced back and forth in the room. She looked periodically at Trill's dead body which made her quiver each time. *Please pick up… please pick up,* she said to herself as the phone rang.

"Hey, Diamond."

"The plan we talked about earlier is canceled. I need you to come to my place *now*! The address is 1347 Dorchester Drive. Hurry! Please!"

"What's going on? Is everything OK?" Officer Burrell asked.

"No! Now hurry!" Diamond told him.

She hung up the phone and asked Naomi to help her run some of her bags for her and the boys to the car. After tonight, Diamond wasn't stepping foot back in this place once she left. Whatever she didn't take, she was leaving. Before Officer Burrell came, she went in Trill's pocket and took the few hundred dollars he had, then she went upstairs to the safe and took a few more stacks that amounted to $4,500.

When they were walking back to the house from putting the things inside of Naomi's car, Officer Burrell pulled up behind them. Diamond and Naomi stood in the front lawn while they waited for him to approach them.

"Hey, ladies."

"Hi, Officer Burrell. This is my best friend, Naomi."

"Nice to meet you," he told Naomi after shaking her hand. "What's going on, ladies?"

"Follow me," Diamond told him.

When Officer Burrell walked in the house, he noticed how much of a mess it was. It was obvious there had been a fight. He wasn't expecting to see Trill lying in blood on the floor. In fact, he thought Diamond would be in that position before him, and he told her just that.

"Thanks to my friend, I'm alive. She saved my life, Officer Burrell."

"Oh, so she pulled the trigger?" he asked.

Naomi handed over her phone to the cop. She recorded Trill telling Diamond the truth about what happened to Rod. Officer Burrell took Naomi's phone and cropped the video, making sure to crop out anything Naomi and Diamond said that could backfire on them.

Officer Burrell walked over to Trill and stood over him.

"It's been a long time coming, brother. You were one sneaky dude. Oh, and really good at what you did too, but I knew your time was coming sooner or later," he told him.

He took a piece of cloth out of his pocket and wiped both guns off then put Trill's fingerprints on both. The gun that shot Trill, he put on the floor near the body. He told Diamond to open her shirt and tossed the gun she had back to her. He told her to put it up in a good spot. She went to the closet where all of his belongings were and buried it in the bag of clothes.

He stood in front of the girls and said, "Looks to me like he couldn't handle a breakup and shot himself because his lover was leaving him. Look at how he abused your face during the fight. You are lucky to still be alive, my friend. He is one dangerous man."

Officer Burrell started to walk off and said, "Naomi, follow me. I'm going to give you this soap out of my car. You take it home and wash your hands really well. This will remove the gun powder. Here's some cash. Take an Uber home, shower with this soap as well, and get rid of everything you have on now. Use your shirt and toss Diamond your keys. Remember, she borrowed your car tonight." He winked.

He reached in his pockets and deleted the video from Naomi's phone and handed it back to her.

"Diamond, did you catch that?"

"All of it!"

"Good! I was in the area and you flagged me down, OK?"

"Got it."

"Now, I need to call this in. You will need to give a statement, so remember what I told you. Everything that happened beforehand, don't mention it. Nobody knew we were working together to capture these guys."

"What about my case with DSS?"

"This will help it for sure." Officer Burrell smiled.

When Naomi left, Diamond sat on the stairs in a daze. She never saw it ending between her and Trill like it did. With just seven months of knowing each other, their time had ended. Although he put her through a lot of shit in just four months of them dating, she didn't regret the journey she had with him. She learned lessons, she gained closure and became much wiser and knowledgeable about the streets, the drug game, and the types of men to avoid. It felt like the end, but it was actually the beginning for her.

Epilogue

A month later

Now that Trill was gone, Diamond was finally focused. She completed her classes and had a clean drug test. Her and Naomi sat in Naomi's apartment, waiting for the boys to be brought back to her.

"The day is here, Diamond. Are you excited?" Naomi asked.

"You damn right I am! Do you think the boys will be happy to see me?"

"I know they will be. Everyone goes through trials and tribulations, but you've always been a great mom."

Diamond and Naomi looked at the time and saw it was five minutes away from their arrival. They went to sit outside while they continued to wait. The time was getting closer, and Diamond instantly felt a knot in the pit of her stomach. She stared every car down that went past, hoping it was them.

"There they are," Naomi told her when the car rolled up and stopped in front of Naomi's place.

Diamond got up from the chair and stood on the porch, looking at the car. Tears filled her eyes as soon as she saw the back door of the car open, and her boys hopped out with their back packs. They ran across the lawn to her, and Diamond met them halfway.

"Maaaa!" Josh yelled.

"Mommaaa!" Jordan screamed.

When they met, Diamond dropped down to her knees and hugged them both tightly. She kissed them on their cheeks and rubbed her hands across their heads.

"Oh, babies! I'm so glad y'all are home. I couldn't wait to see y'all and hold y'all again. I never thought this day would be here with how long it took to come. But I told y'all I was gonna come for y'all, and I did. This will not happen again. Mommy loves the both of you." Diamond sobbed.

Naomi walked over and placed her arms around all of them. Diamond slowly looked up at Naomi and said, "Thank you for everything."

"Auntie MiMi helped me with a lot. Y'all give her some hugs and kisses while I go over here and talk to this young lady," Diamond told the twins.

The boys ran over to Naomi, and she walked them closer to the house away from Diamond and the CPS lady. While Diamond was walking toward her, a black Tahoe with darkly tinted windows pulled up. Diamond stopped. Just because Trill was gone didn't mean they were safe. In fact, word was spreading quickly about what happened to him, so she knew they needed to get away fast. Diamond looked back and saw the boys were good, then she looked back at the truck and glued her eyes to it. Shortly after parking, Officer Burrell hopped out.

Diamond placed one hand over her heart. "Oh, thank God," she whispered.

The CPS lady looked at Diamond and smiled. "How does it feel, Ms. Johnson?"

"Much better than the first time I saw you," Diamond replied.

"I'm sure it does. It's never my intentions to break up a family and hurt them. We strive to protect these children and make sure they are safe, that's all I was trying to do."

"I know. It was upsetting for me to watch the only people I had in my corner get taken away from me after my mom and brother left. Let me apologize to you for the way I acted."

"Thank you for that, but you do not have to apologize for being a loving and concerned mother. Actually, I want you to continue to be the mother that you are but make better choices. Not only for you, but for those kids so we don't have to go through this again. I see you have a visitor, so I will get going now."

The CPS lady shuffled around her purse and pulled out her card.

"Here's my contact information if you need me for anything. Bye now," she told Diamond.

She walked off, and Diamond looked at the card, not noticing that Officer Burrell was now standing near her.

"Hello, Diamond."

She looked up after hearing his deep voice acknowledging her.

"Hey, Officer Burrell. How are you?"

"Call me Maurice. I see you have what you wanted. How does it feel?"

"Amazing. Thank you so much for all that you did for my family and me. I can't thank you enough."

"Just because I'm a cop doesn't mean that I'm an asshole. I do keep promises, make sure that justice is served, and help who I can on and off the clock," he joked.

Diamond blushed for the first time in a long time.

"You have such a beautiful smile." He complimented her.

"Thank you."

"I don't mean any harm or disrespect, but I'd like to take you out for coffee one day."

Diamond looked around as she thought about the best way to respond but also to make sure she didn't later regret the answer that she gave.

"Uh, I don't know. It's so soon."

"It's just a coffee date, but I understand. You have been through a lot these past few months."

"When I'm in town, I will hit you up. How does that sound?"

"Are you leaving?"

"Yeah, we all are. We need a fresh start, you know. Charleston isn't for us anymore. I've gotten what I've needed. Now that Rod can finally rest in peace, I think the boys and I are gonna go live and be free. Thanks to you, we are all able to do that now."

"No problem at all. Take care of yourself and those boys. I'll be here if you decide to come back. If I can visit you by any chance, please let me know."

Diamond smiled and said, "I will."

Maurice started walking off to his truck, then Diamond yelled, "Wait."

Maurice stopped and turned around. Diamond ran to him and gave him a big hug. "Thank you for everything," she told him again then turned him loose, and they each went their separate ways.

Diamond walked to the porch where Naomi and the twins stood, then they all went in the house. The boys immediately noticed the packed boxes and furniture disorganized and scattered.

"What's this?" Josh asked.

"We are moving far away. What do you guys think about that?"

"We're down! It's about time we get away from this crazy place," Jordan said.

Diamond laughed. "You know what, son? I was thinking the exact same thing. And guess what? Auntie MiMi is coming with us," Diamond said to them.

"Yay!" The twins screamed at the top of their lungs.

"What about Mr. Tee?" Jordan asked.

"You just had to ask, didn't you?" Josh replied.

"Calm down, boys. We don't have to worry about him anymore. He's gone for good. Come on. We need to make one last run before we leave tomorrow," Diamond said.

When they got in the car, they drove to Ms. Mable's. The door was closed shut, and that was not what she normally did, especially on a nice, breezy, sunny day like the one they were having. They all stood at the door, waiting for an answer while Diamond pounded on the door as if she was the police.

"Ms. Mable, it's Diamond!" She hollered while she continued to knock.

Josh turned the doorknob. Diamond slapped his hand and fixed her mouth to tell him to get off it, until she realized the knob turned completely and the door was unlocked. Diamond looked at Naomi for suggestions. Naomi shrugged her shoulders, and Diamond stepped inside of the house first.

Nothing was on, and Ms. Mable was nowhere in sight. Diamond walked in the kitchen and told the twins and Naomi to check the rest of the house. Diamond knew Ms. Mable loved to cook and went to check the burners on the stove to see if they were warm like they were recently used. Diamond laid her hand flat across each of them; they were all cold.

She turned around to head out the kitchen and saw a note on the counter for her.

Diamond, we tried getting in contact with you but weren't successful. Call this number and ask for Susanne, Mable's sister.

"Naomi, come here!" she yelled.

"She's not in here, Diamond. The boys and I looked everywhere."

"Yeah, I figured. Look at this though. It was on the counter."

"Call the number," Naomi told her.

Diamond called the number.

"Hi, this is Susanne."

"Um, hi, Susanne. This is Diamond. I got the note on Ms. Mable's counter. Is she with you?"

"I know who you are, baby. Mable talked about you all the time. I have been trying to reach you. She asked me to call you many times before she left. She kept saying she wanted to see you and the boys."

"Where is she? I can come by now. Can I talk to her?"

"I'm afraid not, baby. Mable's gone."

"She's gone? Nooooo! I told her I was coming to see her. I brought the boys." Diamond cried.

"She really tried waiting on y'all. She was hospitalized shortly after you went by to see her last time, but she's been gone for about a month now. She was suffering badly; she couldn't take it anymore. I promised her that I would let you know, but she wanted me to tell you that she loved y'all and to take care of yourselves."

Diamond sat on the chair and sobbed. At that moment, Naomi knew what it was.

Susanne continued. "She left something for you. Go inside the kitchen and slide the refrigerator to the right, away from the cabinets."

Diamond got up and told Naomi to follow and help her.

They pulled the refrigerator and saw an envelope. Diamond grabbed it and looked inside. She saw lots of cash.

"What's this?" Diamond asked Susanne.

"She said she couldn't accept it. She said she saved it in case either you or the boys needed it. Something about you gave it to her some time ago or something."

Diamond grinned. "That's one stubborn lady. I told her it was my way of showing her that the boys and I appreciated her, and I told her to use it for herself. People take advantage of her all the time. She still didn't listen."

"That's Mable," Susanne joked.

"I am upset that I couldn't fulfill her wish and see her one last time, but I appreciate talking to you and you leaving the note for me. I wasn't expecting to come over here to this. When I last visited, I told her I would come back for her and take her with us. I saw how much she struggled in here alone and wanted to take care of her, but I was too late."

"It's OK, baby. You and the boys were truly a blessing to her. Don't beat yourself up about it. We will be cleaning out her place soon, so while you are there, look around and take whatever you'd like."

"Thank you, Susanne. It was nice talking to you."

As soon as Diamond hung up, the boys asked where Ms. Mable was.

"She's gone," Diamond told them.

They wept on the chair while Diamond and Naomi comforted them.

"Lupus took a toll on her. When I was here last, she was weak and getting very thin. She asked about y'all. I just wish we got to her sooner." Diamond continued.

They grabbed a few things to keep her in memory and headed back to Naomi's. Diamond cooked spaghetti and garlic bread while the boys showered. Naomi sat in the living room, flicking through channels to find something to watch. She stopped on the news with interest in the weather. After the weather, they talked about how the police made a huge drug bust. They showed Officer Burrell being applauded for his good work.

"Diamond, come here, quick. Look at this!"

Diamond ran to Naomi. "What is it?"

Naomi pointed at the TV. Diamond sat next to Naomi on the couch and continued to watch. They listened to them talking about how much safer the community will be now that they'd seized the biggest drug organization on the streets. They mentioned one of the head chiefs being dead and the others in custody. They showed Red Man's mugshot and talked about him running drugs through his strip club that was closed down for good. Then Black's mugshot came on the screen and said he was being charged with Rod's murder. Diamond and Naomi looked at each other and smiled.

"We make a damn good team," Diamond said.

"We sure do," Naomi agreed.

The next day, Diamond, Naomi, and the twins went to Georgia where they found a small affordable home. Diamond used the money that she got from Ms. Mable and stole from Trill to help Naomi out with the expenses. Thirteen thousand dollars wasn't much and went extremely fast, but she used it all to help, hoping to get back on her feet soon.

Diamond landed a job at a department store which was paying her a few more dollars an hour than what she made at Burger King. Although she was back where she started, things felt so much better. She was done with dancing and was hoping to further her education to become a social worker.

Naomi, on the other hand, found another strip club and was starting there soon. She was close to having enough money for her salon before things with Trill and Diamond fell apart, but she was going to keep working at the club until she got enough money. She was focused on making her dreams come true, and she was going to shake her ass and gather loose bills until it happened. Now, she was just as desperate for money as Diamond was, but she was determined not to fall in the trap of these dope dealers like she did.

About the Author

Courtney was born and raised in North Charleston, South Carolina, most of her life. She currently resides in a small town outside of North Charleston called Goose Creek, with her son and daughter.

Although she has an Associate's in Health Science and has been in healthcare most of her career, her passion for writing led her to chase her dreams. Courtney has always been thrilled to write and use her imagination, and she has been writing short stories since a young age. As she grew older and experienced more of life, writing became more than just a hobby; she found it therapeutic. As she wrote more, she knew she wanted to be a published author. Courtney has so many stories to tell!

When she isn't reading or turning her imagination into a work of art, she is spending time with her family, in front of a camera, or watching shows she loves, such as *Power*, *Saints and Sinners*, *Hell's Kitchen*, and *The Chi*.

With the links below, you can connect with Courtney for upcoming events, appearances, to purchase books, or simply to give her feedback at:

Instagram: @author_courtneysimone

Facebook: @officialcourtneysimone

Address: P.O. box #446 Goose Creek, SC 29445

For business inquires: contactcourtneys@gmail.com

Amazon author page: amazon.com/author/courtneysimone

www.ingramcontent.com/pod-product-compliance
Lightning Source LLC
Chambersburg PA
CBHW061136200626
46817CB00016B/1655